A Very Happy Halloween

HAPPY EVER AFTER
BOOK THREE

ELISE NOBLE

Published by Undercover Publishing Limited

v2

ISBN: 978-1-912888-91-7

Edited by Nikki Mentges, NAM Editorial

Cover design by Elise Noble

www.undercover-publishing.com

www.elise-noble.com

The doctor crouched in front of us. Grey hair and glasses gave him a reassuring air of experience, but if he'd spent his life working in this place, he was probably more like thirty than fifty-five. My sister's fiancé was a doctor, only twenty-six, but he was already starting to look a bit worn down.

"What seems to be the problem, son?"

"Anvil de Witt pushed me."

"I see. Well, let's take a look at you."

"My wrist hurts."

"We're going to fix that. Have you ever been in a hospital before?"

"Yes, when I was born," Alfie said earnestly. "And when I was two, I put peas up my nose, and when I was two and a half, popcorn got stuck in my ear, and when I was three—"

My phone rang. *Oh, thank goodness.* Saved by technology, right before Alfie could tell everyone in A&E about the "black balls" incident, although perhaps the doctor already knew? Liam—Marissa's fiancé—had spilled the details over dinner one night, practically crying with laughter, and he worked at a hospital two hours away. Of course, he didn't realise that I was the "hysterical mother" who'd thought her three-year-old had some weird tropical disease when all he'd done was colour his testicles with a felt tip. In my defence, I'd never had any of that drama with Harry. Until the split, he'd always been the easy child.

I glanced at the phone screen, hoping for Harry but seeing Steven's name flash up instead. About bloody time.

"I'm so sorry. It's my husband."

My husband. The words left a nasty taste in my mouth, but over the past few months, I'd realised just how much meaning they held. "My husband" meant you were a fine, upstanding member of the community. "Alfie's dad" left people wondering why I was divorced or whether I hadn't been good enough to marry in the first place. Folks didn't say as much, of course, but I saw it in their eyes. And referring to my not-quite-ex as "the arsehole sperm donor" made them pass gin and tissues.

Today, I didn't need judgment. I just needed Alfie's arm fixed so I could go home and drink my own alcohol.

The doctor waved a hand. "No problem. Worried about young Alfie, is he?"

"He's at work," I said, as if that answered everything.

The doctor motioned to us to follow him, and I stabbed at the screen to answer the call as we headed for a set of double doors that led deeper into the hospital.

"What's Alfie done this time?" was Steven's opening line.

"He hasn't *done* anything. A boy pushed him over in the playground, and now his wrist is sore and swollen."

"Well, I hope you put in a complaint."

"Between finishing up at work and bringing him to the hospital, I've been a little busy. Can you look after Harry this evening? He went home with a boy in his class, but I barely know Shawn's mum, and I'm worried."

Mainly because she wasn't answering the phone either.

"I'm on my way to a work dinner. Can't your mum pick him up?"

"I told you my parents are on a cruise this month."

"Who goes on a cruise for a month?"

"It was a treat from Marissa."

Tokyo to Seattle via Alaska, Mum's dream trip. She and Dad had been looking forward to it for months. Their absence meant I'd needed to cut down on appointments at the salon for a few weeks, but how could I complain about them taking a much-deserved break?

"Can't Marissa take care of Harry?"

"She lives a hundred miles away, and you know she

4

hates driving on the motorway." And besides, Marissa wasn't Harry's father; Steven was. Just for once, couldn't he lift a finger to help? "Can't you back out of the dinner?"

"I need to make a living, Janie."

"So you can carry on not paying child support?"

"The judge hasn't set an amount yet."

"So? Why should that stop you from contributing?"

"I do contribute. I buy them stuff and look after them at the weekends."

"You look after them every other weekend, and you buy them phones and computer games when what they need is food and PE kit. Do you even know how much school uniforms cost?"

"I don't have time for this right now," he said in that whiny "you're being unreasonable" voice of his.

Neither did I. The doctor was holding open a cubicle curtain, waiting for me, and there was no point in arguing with Steven. He wouldn't change his mind. Once, I'd found his tenacity attractive, but now I realised he was just a stubborn git.

"Fine. Keep shirking your responsibilities, but don't come crying to me when your bad decisions bite you in the arse."

"Janie, that's not fair—"

I ended the call and hurried to catch up with Alfie and the doctor. The corridor smelled strongly of cleaning products, but even the floral scent couldn't cover up the faint underlying aroma of vomit. I hated this. Hated it. Not just that Alfie was injured, but that my life wasn't my own anymore. Ever since I'd found the empty condom wrapper in Steven's pocket, things had fallen apart. He'd moved in with Luisa, who was not only his bit on the side but my boss —ex-boss, now—while I'd lost my job, my home, and my sanity. If it weren't for my sister, I'd probably be living in a shop doorway.

Alfie needed an X-ray, which meant more waiting. And more worrying. What was the point in having mobile phones if people never answered them? I desperately wanted to call Marissa, to hear a friendly voice and for her to offer to drop everything and drive to Somerset to help. She would, I knew she would. Which was ridiculous because I was the older sister. I was supposed to be the capable, responsible one. And until the condom incident, I'd lived up to those expectations. Yes, I'd had a couple of wild years in my teens, but after being ghosted by one tattooed bad boy, cheated on by another hot jackass, and then fished out of the gutter by a virtual stranger when I tried to erase the memories of my poor decisions with alcohol poisoning, I'd settled down. I'd met a nice, respectable man with a nice, respectable job. Steven worked in the finance department at a software company, no ink or piercings in sight. Okay, so my first pregnancy hadn't exactly been planned, but we'd made it work. Steven had proposed, and we'd married in a beautiful ceremony at a country hotel. Everyone said we made a lovely couple. We shared a dream honeymoon in Antigua, I quit my office job and retrained as a hairdresser so I could flex my hours around childcare, and we moved into a dull but sturdy semi-detached home on the outskirts of Bristol.

Life was perfect.

Slightly boring, perhaps, but my only worries had been what to cook for dinner and whether Alfie had stashed any more creepy-crawlies in his bedroom. Steven said it was a phase and I should let him grow out of it, but Steven wasn't the one left picking snails off the curtains.

No, Marissa had been the daughter our parents worried about. They'd never discussed it with me, of course, but once or twice, I'd overheard them whispering about whether

her latest loser boyfriend was taking advantage of her the way his predecessors had. Whether it had been wise of her to leave Engleby on a whim with no real plan for where she wanted to go in life. Whether she was just too *nice*. Then she'd hooked up with a dishy doctor and won the bloody lottery, in that order, and now I was the one they whispered about.

I was thrilled for my sister, really I was, but sometimes, seeing her happiness made me want to weep.

Maybe that was why I hadn't called her right away? Because I didn't want to be reminded, yet again, of my own inadequacies?

I dialled Harry's number, beyond relieved when he finally picked up.

"Harry, why didn't you answer when I called before? I've been worried."

"Harry?" The voice was deep and raspy, and it definitely didn't belong to my son. My stomach knotted in an instant. "So that's his name."

"W-w-who are you?" I stuttered. "Who are you, and where's my son?"

Two

"Your son?" the stranger asked. "I don't know where he is now, but forty minutes ago, he was throwing red paint over my front door."

What?

"Are you crazy? Harry would never—" I started, but then I stopped. A year ago, I'd have been confident in that assertion, but since the separation, my older son had changed. I did my best to avoid arguing with Steven in front of the boys, but they picked up on the animosity between us, especially Harry. He was more sensitive than Alfie. A born worrier. Mum said he needed stability, and I'd struggled to provide that these past few months.

And Steven's idea of parenting was to bribe the kids into behaving, so now when they didn't get their own way, they'd begun acting out. The days after Steven had taken them for the weekend were always particularly challenging. Would Harry have done something dumb in a quest for attention? I couldn't entirely rule it out.

But I couldn't rule it in either. He was at Shawn's house. Shawn's mother was supposed to be supervising him.

And then there was the fact that the man on the phone was a total stranger. This could be a wind-up. What if he'd found the phone, and now he was trying to extort money out of me?

"He dropped the phone as he ran off," the man said, and his voice wouldn't have been entirely unpleasant under different circumstances. "You want me to send you the video?"

There was a video? Fantastic. But what if Harry's phone had been stolen prior to the paint incident? Bullies had been a problem at school, and Harry was small for his age, so it wouldn't have been difficult for one of the little monsters in his class to take it. Maybe this was all a case of mistaken identity?

The doctor pulled back the cubicle curtain. "Mrs. Osman?"

"I'm going to have to call you back," I told the paint-scammer guy.

"Are you kidding—"

I disconnected the call and forced myself to take a steadying breath as I decided whether to scream, cry, or throw up. You know the exploding-head emoji? Well, it was like looking into a mirror.

"Do I get a cast?" Alfie asked. "Mason James had a cast, and we all wrote our names on it."

"Well, you get a partial cast," the doctor said. "Not so good for writing names, but you can take it off in the bath."

"Our bathroom broke. We have to go to Grandma's if we want a shower."

"Just a little water leak." I tried to make light of the situation. "We're waiting for the plumber to come."

The good plumber. I'd already tried one idiot, and he'd made the problem worse, not better. Mariusz, the guy everyone recommended, couldn't fit us in until four weeks from Tuesday, which meant shuttling back and forth between Marigold Lodge and my parents' place with sleepy boys and bottles of shampoo.

"Oh dear."

"Does Alfie have a break? Or is it just a sprain?"

"We call it a buckle fracture. Young bones are quite flexible, so rather than cracking straight through, they tend to bend instead." The doctor put Alfie's X-ray on a lightbox to show us. "See this small bulge here?"

I did. "How long will it take to heal?"

"Three weeks or so. He can take ibuprofen for any pain, and if the swelling doesn't go down, pop in to see your GP." The doctor ruffled Alfie's hair. "No more playground shenanigans."

"I'm not going back to school. It sucks."

Oh, please no. The doctor gave me a sympathetic look and backed away.

"School's important, son. Sit tight, and a nurse will come through with a splint shortly."

Alfie watched me carefully, ready for the argument, but I just couldn't. Not here, not now. If Alfie had a meltdown in A&E, I was the one who'd end up hospitalised. Although I couldn't lie—a nice rest in the psychiatric ward did hold a certain appeal. No laundry to do, no homework, no checking that Harry hadn't found his way around the parental controls on the internet again. Steven would have to take care of the boys, and— No, that was a terrible idea. Someone groaned, and I realised it was me.

"We'll talk about this later."

"But—"

"Later."

It was Friday. Which meant I could kick the can down the road for two days, and by Sunday, maybe Alfie would have changed his mind? It wasn't as if he liked being at home much, anyway.

When we moved to Engleby, there had been two properties for sale in the village—a two-bedroom flat above the local funeral home, and Marigold Lodge. At first, Harry had voted for the flat because he thought it would be cool to see dead bodies being wheeled in and out, but then he realised he'd have to share a room with Alfie and changed his mind. Alfie had voted for Marigold Lodge because of the bug potential in the garden. And me? I'd had the idea that by renovating the place, we could increase the value as a way to thank Marissa for bailing us out of the massive hole we'd found ourselves in.

Marigold Lodge was a four-bedroom, one-and-a-half-bathroom cottage set in an acre of brambles. The roof leaked, and the pipes leaked. Only a handful of the rooms were habitable, so Harry had ended up sharing with Alfie after all, a fact that pleased neither of them. And I'd spent the past five months cursing, crying, evicting spiders, and moving buckets around every time it rained.

The weather forecast over the weekend? Sunshine and showers.

Alfie went into a sulk as I tried calling Shawn's mum yet again. This time, she finally answered.

"Where's Harry? Is he there?"

The woman gave a throaty laugh. "Easy, love. Course he's here. Where else would he be? You haven't picked him up yet."

"Sorry. I'm so sorry. It's just that he's not answering his phone, and then you weren't answering either, so I... Sorry."

"I always turn the ringer off when I'm watching *Whispers in Willowbrook*. You missed a good episode tonight. Detective Cartwright found—"

"Could I just speak to Harry? Please?"

A sigh. "Hold on a sec. The boys are playing on Shawn's Xbox."

I heard rustling as she walked through the house, cursing as she tripped over something, and finally, the sound of shooting. *Dammit, tell me she hasn't let Harry play some eighteen-rated war game.*

"Your mam wants to speak to you," she told him, and the game paused.

The next voice was Harry's. "Mum?"

"Why didn't you answer your phone? I was worried about you."

A long pause. "I lost it."

"You lost your phone?"

"Yeah?"

"Where did you lose it?"

I heard a voice in the background. "If he knew that, he wouldn't've lost it, would he?"

Was that Shawn? Should I be discouraging this particular friendship? Harry was developing enough of an attitude under Steven's influence without others egging him on.

"Where did you last see it?" I tried.

"Don't tell her," Alfie yelled. "She's really mad."

Give me strength.

"I'm not mad," I lied. "It's just been a difficult day."

"School, probably," Harry said. "I had it in physics."

I wanted to believe him. I did. Life would be so much easier if he was telling the truth. Harry could survive without a phone for a week or two, and then Steven would give him a half-hearted lecture and buy a new one. Sure, Steven would inevitably whine that I'd disabled the "Find your gadget" app on the missing device, but if he hadn't been using it to spy on us, I wouldn't have had to. We'd fight, I'd slam the door in his face, and things would carry on as normal. The paint-on-door stranger could go and scam somebody else.

There was just one teensy problem with all that.

Harry was lying.

Three

Harry didn't lie often, but when he did, he got a slight tremor in his voice that was a dead giveaway. Such as the time he claimed he hadn't done his homework because he felt sick the whole weekend, but then it turned out that Steven and Luisa had taken both boys to a music festival on Saturday, and on Sunday, they'd all gone go-karting. Steven had posted about it on Facebook. I'd blocked him, of course, but then my divorce lawyer told me we needed to keep an eye on his spending, so I'd set up a new profile for "Martha Fokker," added a picture of a random blonde with plenty of cleavage, and waited three point five seconds for Steven to click the "Accept friend request" button. So far, I'd watched him buy a new Jaguar, gift Luisa a pair of diamond earrings, and take a holiday to the Algarve, all with money he claimed he didn't have. To be fair, that might have been true. He was a big fan of credit cards.

Annnnnnd I was getting angry again...

Deep breaths.

The hospital wasn't the place for this battle, and nor was it sensible to call Harry out over the phone. Firstly, Shawn's

14

mum would be there to witness my parenting fail, and secondly, my darling son would be able to hang up on me.

"Well, Alfie's almost done here, and I'll pick you up as soon as I can."

"It's fine. Shawn's mum said she'd order pizza."

Pizza? Then of course he'd want to stay. Pizza was a rare treat for us, usually when Marissa came over with Liam. But if I had to pay to replace a stranger's door, then Harry would be on a pizza ban for, say, the next decade.

"Promise me you'll be good."

He did promise, and then he hung up, and I sat in the chair beside Alfie's bed wondering if his brother had just told me another lie. This was hard, so hard. Most of the popular parenting blogs conveniently left out the depression and despair and focused on crafts, fun days out, and ways to keep your home perfect with kids around. Even the sites that touched on the downsides thought yoga and mindfulness was the answer. How was I supposed to shepherd two boys towards adulthood when some days, I barely had the energy to get out of bed?

Honestly, I'd wanted to stop at one child, but Steven had worn me down over the years. He'd been so lonely growing up, he said. He'd always wished for a sibling, so it would be cruel to deprive Harry of that joy. My second pregnancy had been even worse than the first. Months of puking and waddling, followed by twelve hours of labour and a torn perineum. And the worst part? Steven had missed the actual birth thanks to a work call, then arrived back in time to take an unflattering picture of me with tear-streaked cheeks and hair plastered to my face and post it on his LinkedIn account with the caption "We just had a baby boy!"

We?

We?

I could cope with the pain, but not with that asshat taking credit for my hard work. One minute of pleasure for him, nine months of discomfort for me. The moment the painkillers wore off, I'd booked an appointment to have my tubes tied. Steven had grumbled about that, but when I pointed out that the alternative was him having a vasectomy, he quickly agreed.

And then went out to wet the baby's head with his buddies.

After I threw a bedpan at him—the nurse told me I had great aim—he'd promised to help more with the children, but of course, he'd broken that promise within two weeks of Alfie's birth. While I dealt with housework and baby colic, he went on a golfing weekend with his work pals and then escaped to the office for twelve hours a day. My worst nightmare was that Harry would grow up and turn into his father.

But I couldn't turn back the clock.

And nor could I avoid calling the stranger whose property Harry had most likely damaged earlier this evening. If nothing else, I needed to get the facts straight before I confronted Harry later. And when I said "confront," I meant in a positive and constructive way, obviously.

"Mum, I'm hungry," Alfie said.

So was I. Starving. I'd run out of time for breakfast after Harry spilled Rice Krispies all over the floor, and then missed lunch thanks to Alfie's accident.

"I'll see if I can find a vending machine. You stay right here, okay?"

"Okay."

The vending machine in the alcove off the waiting room dispensed one cereal bar, then promptly ate the rest of my change and flashed up an error code. The lady behind the desk, who looked almost as harried as I felt, offered to call the maintenance team. Her grimace suggested they wouldn't be along any time soon.

Great.

But with the machine out of action, the alcove did offer a quiet spot to call the stranger, and I gave a heavy sigh as I dialled Harry's phone again. At least I was prepared this time.

He answered almost immediately. "Thought you were going to ghost me."

"Look, I'm having a really bad day, so can we just get this over with?"

"Sure." He sounded remarkably agreeable. "Give me your number. You show up as 'Mum' on your boy's phone."

Thankfully, Harry had set a PIN, so at least this stranger couldn't snoop through private photos and contacts. Small mercies. A part of me wanted to tell the man to keep the phone, hang up, and pretend Harry hadn't snuck out while Shawn's mum watched *Whispers in Willowbrook*. Steven would have done exactly that. But unfortunately, my parents had drilled some morals into me, so I read out my number.

"This had better not be a scam. If you send me porn, I'm calling the police."

"Yeah, I imagine you're the type of woman who would."

"What's that supposed to mean? 'Type of woman'?"

"You sound a little uptight."

"Uptight? I'm not— Okay, fine. I'm uptight. But so would you be if one of your children was in the hospital and the other was busy vandalising private property. I'm not saying he did," I added hastily. "Just that it's a possibility."

"What's wrong with your other kid?"

"He broke his arm. His wrist. The doctor called it a buckle fracture."

"Relax—he'll be right as rain in a couple of weeks."

"How do you know?" Curiosity got the better of me. "Did you ever break your wrist?"

"Twice that I know of, plus I had a buckle fracture in my tibia from jumping off my grandma's balcony. Superhero movies have a lot to answer for."

"Well, Alfie wasn't watching superhero movies. A boy in his class pushed him over in the playground, which is another problem because he's never been one for confrontation, and—" Wait. Why was I talking to a complete stranger about my problems? Although *was* he a complete stranger? There was a niggling familiarity about his voice, and I thought I might have bumped into him around the village at some point. "Can you just send me the bloody video?"

He gave an irritating chuckle. "Sure, sweetheart."

Sweetheart? I wasn't his freaking sweetheart. Beads of sweat popped out on the back of my neck as I waited. Was the door salvageable? If not, how much did a new one cost? I was about to google when my phone buzzed.

Show time.

The video was every bit as awful as I'd feared. Worse, even. The doorbell camera had recorded Harry struggling up the steps wearing a pair of mittens and his Spider-Man Halloween mask, lugging what had to be a five-litre can of paint. There was a pause as he used a screwdriver to lever the lid open, and then he tossed the contents at the front door, took a picture of his handiwork, and hotfooted it down the drive. But he couldn't have tucked his phone very far into his pocket because it bounced onto the lawn as he ran, and in the last seconds of the clip, I spotted a boy wearing a royal-blue sweatshirt duck out of the bushes and follow him. Shawn? Maybe it wasn't only Steven who was a bad influence.

A sigh escaped. I'd been so relieved when Harry started

making friends at the new school that I hadn't stopped to wonder whether they were the right kind of friends.

I called the stranger back, on his own phone this time.

"Fine, how much is a door?"

"Oh, I don't want you to fix it."

"You don't?"

"Nah, your kid is going to fix it himself."

"What?"

"You can supervise."

Was he joking? Harry was eleven years old. He didn't know the first thing about doors.

"A professional would do a much better job."

"And all your kid would learn is that when he fucks up, his mum will bail him out. You need to teach him a different lesson—that he has to be responsible for his own mistakes. How do you think he'd do in a young offenders' institution?"

I gasped. "Prison?"

"If you won't teach him the consequences of his actions, someone else will have to."

My guts churned at the thought. I didn't want Harry to become *that* boy, the one everyone rolled their eyes when they spoke about. The one people went out of their way to avoid. And I definitely didn't want things escalating enough that juvenile detention was a possibility.

"He'll come and wash the door tomorrow morning."

The boys had been looking forward to a day out—swimming followed by a trip to the cinema—but swimming was a no-go thanks to Alfie's cast, and now we'd have to cancel the movie too. Harry would just have to apologise to Alfie as well as the man whose property he'd damaged. Righting wrongs took precedence. What if Harry hadn't dropped his phone? What if the stranger had called the police instead? We'd all be in a whole world of trouble.

"Washing won't work. It was gloss paint. The door needs sanding down and repainting, the doorstep too. Plus he'll need to use his allowance to buy a new doormat."

More money that I didn't have. I bit back a groan. "We'll go to the hardware store first. Will eleven-ish work?"

"Eleven is fine."

"Thanks for being so understanding about all this, uh... I didn't get your name?"

"You can call me Chip."

"Chip?"

"Is there a problem with that?"

"Uh, no? No problem." The name didn't match the voice, that was all. With that gravelly timbre, he sounded like the hero from a romance novel, and romance-novel heroes weren't called Chip. Maybe that was why his voice seemed familiar? I did listen to a lot of audiobooks. "Where do you live? I mean, where should we come to paint the door?"

"Your son can give you the answer to that question."

Harry would tell me? Great. One more difficulty on top of the eleventy million I was already dealing with, but Chip didn't strike me as the type of man who would bend in an argument.

"Wish me luck."

"What should I call you?"

"Janie. I'm Janie. And I guess we'll see you tomorrow."

His soft chuckle sent a ripple of something dark and sinful through me.

"Good luck, Janie."

Four

"Harry sucks, Harry sucks, Harry got told off," Alfie sang as he rode around the hardware store on the trolley. I didn't particularly like him riding on the trolley, but if I made him walk, he'd only wander off. Harry was dragging his heels behind us with a face like a winter thundercloud.

"Alfie, don't be rude to your brother."

"Why not? It's his fault we have to paint stuff at the creepy haunted house. I want to watch a movie. You said I could have popcorn."

The discussion with Harry had gone about as well as I'd figured it would. At first, he'd denied everything, which was a trick he'd probably learned from Shawn, who'd learned it from his mother. When I arrived to pick Harry up last night, I'd broached the subject of the boys' excursion with her while Harry used the loo, and she'd flat-out denied it had happened. Even when I showed her the video, she'd assured me that "Shawn would never do something like that." Shawn had stood behind her, smirking in his royal-blue sweatshirt, and I realised I needed to find a backup babysitter, fast.

"If you both behave, we can go to the cinema next week."

"Why can't I go to Dad's house? I don't want to watch Harry paint stuff."

"Dad's helping Luisa to fix a water leak at the salon today."

There, that sounded better than "Dad's helping Luisa to find her tonsils and doesn't want to be interrupted." I didn't believe the water leak excuse at all. Not only was Steven useless at DIY, but Luisa's cousin was also a plumber.

"I don't like Luisa. She flushed Harry down the loo."

"She did *what*?" I turned to Harry. "Is this true?"

"He means Harry the woodlouse," Harry the human said. "Alfie was keeping him in the plastic thingy from a Kinder egg."

"I made air holes," Alfie said indignantly. "And I gave him pencil shavings to eat."

"Alfie cried for, like, an hour."

"I did not!"

For Pete's sake. "I'll ask your dad to make sure Luisa puts the woodlouse outside next time."

And there would be a next time, I was sure of it.

"Why couldn't I just keep him?"

"Because a plastic capsule isn't a good home for a living creature."

"So can we make a better home?"

Boy, I'd walked right into that one. "We have to fix up our own place first."

Harry made a gagging noise. "Yeah, if I have to share a bedroom with Alfie, he's not putting creepy-crawlies in there."

"Let's talk about this later, okay?" I'd kicked so many

cans down the road at this point, my toes were bruised. "We need to find sandpaper, paint, brushes, undercoat, gloss, and white spirit."

I'd spent last night lying awake, googling paint removal techniques, and come to the conclusion that Chip was right —the door needed to be repainted. And after I updated Steven on the situation, he'd texted to say that it wasn't our problem, that Harry's face wasn't even visible in the video so the police wouldn't have enough evidence to prosecute, and the guy should claim on his insurance. He hadn't offered to buy so much as a paintbrush.

When we had the Big Talk last night, Harry's face had crumpled when he realised there was a video, and he'd sniffed back tears when I told him that he had to make good on the damage. Shawn had dared him to throw paint at the creepy old haunted house on the hill, apparently. Yes, Shawn was definitely a bad influence.

As for the house, I couldn't disagree with the description. Marissa and I used to give Twilight's End a wide berth when we were kids. Some of the boys from school had snuck in—to ring the bell and run away, not to throw paint —but I'd never dared to cross the fence line. The place was a huge old gothic mansion, hidden away at the edge of the village, not too far from the new housing estate where Shawn's family lived. The boys had taken a shortcut along a bridleway to get there.

After Harry's reluctant confession, I'd called Marissa to see whether she knew anything about the man who lived there now. *Chip.* As far as I recalled, a rich old crone used to call the place home. Or rather, "second home." She'd never been around much, and she certainly didn't slum it with us regular folks in the village. Marissa had no idea who lived there these days. Mum might have the gossip, but if I called her to ask, she'd want to know why, and I didn't want to ruin her holiday by crying through the phone.

The paint aisle stretched into infinity, and I realised that fifty shades of grey had been a conservative estimate.

"What colour was the door?" I asked Harry.

He shrugged. "Black? Or blue?"

Gee, that was helpful. Okay, we'd buy the basics, work out what we still needed—because there was no way I wouldn't forget something—and come back to get the rest later. My credit card was going to hate me this month. I needed to check in with my lawyer again, but every time she wrote a letter to Steven, it cost me two hundred pounds, and I didn't have two hundred pounds, so I'd been putting it off.

Finally, we had what we needed, and both boys helped —grudgingly—to carry the bags to the bus. My next driving test was booked for three weeks from Tuesday, but the way I felt right now, I might as well cancel it. Every time I took the wheel beside the examiner, I panicked, which meant I made mistakes, which meant I failed. Seven times and counting. When the boys weren't around and I didn't need to carry shopping, I rode a moped, and in Bristol, that had always been enough because Steven drove. But now? Now, I knew the bus timetable by heart, and I had the number of every local cab firm saved in my phone as a backup.

The bus wound its way back to Engleby, past Marigold Lodge, past the parade of shops, past a group of horses, one of whom skittered sideways on the road. Past the primary school, past the church where I made my biggest mistake, past the Hand and Flowers, where I'd made my second-biggest mistake. Past the entrance to the rambler's car park, past the chocolate box cottage I'd always dreamed of living in, past the turnoff to the nature reserve where I'd lost my virginity to an arsehole.

Good memories, bad memories.

At the time of the whole Hand-and-Flowers-nature-reserve disaster, teenage me had thought the world was ending, but now I understood. It had merely been a lesson that all men were bastards. At least Eyes had only blocked my number afterwards. He hadn't left me high and dry with two young children. Plus he'd known what to do with his fingers, tongue, and dick, a concept Steven had struggled with throughout the whole of our eleven-year marriage.

The bus stop was a quarter of a mile from Twilight's End, but the driver was a regular, and I think he felt sorry for me, so he bent the rules and dropped us off right outside with a cheery wave. I felt sick. The gates were ten feet high, imposing metal monstrosities that made the place seem more like a prison than a home, but the intercom was modern.

"The miscreant has come to pay penance," I said to the box.

"You can park outside the door."

"I can't park anywhere since I don't have a bloody car."

"Mum said a bad word," Alfie sang.

"What's a miscreant?" Harry asked.

Chip was probably rolling his eyes. "Then I guess you're in for a walk."

Five

I should have sweet-talked the bus driver into taking us all the way to the front door. Not only was the driveway ridiculously long, but it was also on a hill, and my legs were burning by the time we reached the house. *House.* That made it sound so ordinary. Twilight's End was an enormous grey mansion with arched windows and intricate stonework, heavy on the gargoyles. The door was set back in a porch, and I could see why Chip was upset. Harry had done a thorough job with the paint. The door was splattered, as were the door frame, the doormat, the stone floor, and a small wooden bench that sat to one side. Looked as if we wouldn't be going on any fun trips out for the foreseeable future.

A few bits and pieces sat on the bench—a packet of sandpaper, a tin of black paint, two unused brushes, and a drop cloth. Which was good, because I'd completely forgotten we'd need a drop cloth.

I rang the bell and smiled for the camera.

Okay, maybe it was more of a grimace.

"We're here."

Chip must have been waiting because he answered a second later. "I found some leftover paint in the garage. Best of luck."

"Harry wants to apologise for his error in judgment."

"Wants" was perhaps too strong a word. I'd promised to withhold TV privileges if he didn't say he was sorry, and do it with grace.

"I'm listening."

Chip wasn't going to open the door? That was...weird, but I heard a dog bark somewhere in the house, so possibly he was worried about it escaping? I nudged Harry forward.

"Sorry I threw the paint," he said.

"Make it right, and we'll forget about it. Where's your partner in crime?"

"I dunno."

"Then you need to find better friends, buddy. You might not think it's cool to do what your mum says, but it's even worse having to follow a judge's orders. Got it?"

Harry nodded, and Chip was clearly watching us through the camera.

"Good. If you need water or a bathroom, follow the path on the left to the stable yard."

That was it. Chip just left us there to get on with it, although I swore I could feel him spying on us at times. At least if he turned out to be a serial killer, Marissa knew where we were. And truth be told, there were worse ways to spend a Saturday. Harry was busy sanding, Alfie was lying on the front lawn with a magnifying glass, hunting for bugs, and I'd brought a book.

Unlike the boys, I wasn't heartbroken about missing a trip to the cinema. Bankrupting myself to buy a tub of popcorn while playing referee for the inevitable argument about what to watch was something I could live without. As for swimming, stretch marks and a two-baby pooch had left me feeling self-conscious in a swimsuit, but since seven-year-olds weren't allowed in the water unsupervised, I had to suck it up and squeeze into a one-piece whenever we went to the pool. Plus there was the fact that Alfie swam about as well as I drove, so on an ordinary weekend, I needed to watch him like a hawk in case he tried to sneak onto the diving board.

But this was no ordinary weekend. All in all, sitting on the front steps getting lost in the latest Electi adventure made for a reasonably relaxing morning, even if vacuuming was never far from my mind. And Chip had been remarkably fair when it came to the vandalism. He'd even left Harry's phone under the drop cloth, although I'd pocketed the device before Harry got the chance to grab it. If he wanted it back, he'd have to earn it.

Boy, would he have to earn it.

The weather was forecast to chill off next week, but this afternoon, we had sunshine and a light breeze, and if I blocked out Harry's background muttering and the black clouds scudding across the horizon, I could almost imagine I was on holiday. And that I didn't have two loads of laundry and a leaking roof waiting for me when I got home.

"This is so boring," Harry grumbled.

"It's good practice for when you have to paint your bedroom."

"What?"

"When the roof's fixed and you move into your own room. Fixing up Marigold Lodge is a team effort."

"Dad doesn't make me paint stuff. He pays a guy to do that."

On credit, no doubt. Steven had handled our finances, and until we split up, I hadn't realised that we'd been living beyond our means for years. Nor had I been aware of the two credit cards he'd maxed out in my name. Marissa had come to my rescue and paid off the balances, and now I owed my sister more money than I'd ever be able to afford. She told me not to worry about it, but the guilt kept me awake at night. Should I try to keep my constant anxiety hidden from the boys? Or should I be more open with them about our precarious financial situation?

"Well, we're going to do everything ourselves. It'll be fun. What colour do you want your room to be?"

"Black."

"Black? That's very dark."

"So?"

Did it really matter what colour Harry chose? If living in a cave would make him happy, I could go along with that.

"Okay, black it is."

By the time it began to get dark, Harry had sanded away all the gloss, and I'd given in and helped to pick red spots off the stone floor of the porch. Chip didn't grace us with his presence, so quality control was down to me, and I helped out with the top part of the door that Harry was too short to reach.

I sent Chip a message.

ME

Everything is sanded, and we're going to varnish the bench and undercoat the door tomorrow. But I think we'll have to come back for the gloss.

He replied almost immediately, as if he'd been waiting. Watching. That strange current of energy that had been running through me all day ratcheted up a notch.

CHIP

Next weekend is fine.

ME

> The boys are with their dad next
> weekend, so it'll have to be the weekend
> after or an evening.

A long pause.

CHIP

> Does that mean you're not with their dad?

Why would he ask that? Was he planning to murder us all and checking whether we'd be missed? Or was he just silently judging like so many others? Last week, one of the mums at school had told me boys needed a man in their life to stop them from going off the rails.

ME

> We're talking about the door.

CHIP

> The weekend after or an evening is fine.
> Just let me know what you decide and I'll
> leave the stuff out.

ME

> The weekend after. The boys have school
> during the week, plus my sister is coming
> over.

There. Now he knew someone would look for our bodies. My life might be officially in the crapper, but I still had my family.

His next message didn't arrive until late in the evening, after I'd fed the boys, after I'd hung up the laundry, after I'd checked the weather forecast and made sure the buckets were in place.

CHIP

> Sleep well, Janie.

Sleep well? What was that supposed to mean? Was it merely a friendly text from a man who wasn't a friend? Or was it a veiled threat? Honestly, both options creeped me out. It was definitely inappropriate.

Sleep well?

I barely slept at all that night.

Six

It was Sunday when everything fell apart.

Sunday when I decided to help Harry with the painting because the drying time for the undercoat was four hours, and if we pushed on, we could get the gloss done as well. Then we wouldn't have to spend any extra time around Chip, and I could block his number if he sent me another weird "goodnight" message.

Sunday when I glanced up to check Alfie wasn't digging in Chip's lawn with his yogurt spoon again and found him missing.

"Alfie," I called, but there was no answer, and I cursed under my breath as I stepped out of the porch to look for him. "Alfie, you need to stay in sight."

There was no sign of him. I squinted down the old cobbled driveway, but the only movement was a crow pecking at the neatly mown grass alongside.

"I bet he went to the loo," Harry said. "He drank nearly a whole carton of OJ this morning, remember?"

A sore point for Harry because he'd also wanted orange juice, and there was none left.

"I'm going to check around the back. Don't leave the porch, okay? And call me if Alfie comes back."

"Whatever."

But Alfie wasn't in the toilet. He wasn't in the stable yard, period. The old loose boxes were bolted shut from the outside, and when I checked the smaller doors that looked as if they led to storage rooms, every single one was padlocked shut.

"Alfie!"

Silence.

That all-too-familiar sense of panic welled up inside me. I'd felt it seven months ago when I realised what that condom wrapper in Steven's pocket meant, and again soon after we moved into Marigold Lodge when I first saw water torrenting through the roof. But this was worse.

This was my son.

He couldn't have gone far; logic told me that.

But then I glanced towards the house and saw the side door open.

Shit.

If there was one place a curious seven-year-old like Alfie would go, it was where he wasn't supposed to.

Should I sneak in after him? Or call Chip the possible pervert? Neither option appealed, but leaving Alfie alone to wreak havoc wasn't an option.

I fished my phone out of my pocket and dialled.

"Everything okay?" Chip asked. "Did you run out of paint?"

"I can't find Alfie. He was right by the porch, and then... I don't know. But I saw your side door is open, and—"

"I'll take a look. Primrose probably opened it."

"Who's Primrose?"

A wife? A girlfriend? A housekeeper? Could she help

with the search? Whichever, I felt better knowing there was a woman in the house.

"My dog."

Oh.

"You named your dog Primrose?"

I knew I shouldn't judge, but he sounded like the type of man whose pet would be called Butch or Rambo or Fang. *Primrose?*

"My grandma picked the name. Don't worry if you see her around—she's friendly."

"Your grandma?"

"No, the dog. My grandma's dead."

Crap. "Uh, I'm sorry for your loss."

As well as the house and the stable yard, there was a vast walled area that might have been an old kitchen garden, but the only door I could see that led inside was securely locked. Outside the walls lay acres of parkland dotted with trees, and beyond the parkland was a forest rich with the reds, yellows, and browns of autumn.

"Alfie!"

I stood more chance of finding a competent plumber with immediate availability than I did of locating my son in this sprawling estate. Could he be hiding? I wouldn't have put it past him. He'd grown bored yesterday, and he hadn't been keen on coming back today. Wait, what if he'd followed Primrose? He liked dogs.

I called Chip again.

"Any luck?" he asked.

"Not yet. You?"

"Same, but the house has thirty-seven rooms, so..."

"Is the dog with you? Primrose?"

"No."

"Alfie likes dogs. If he saw her..."

"He might have followed? Got it. I can track the dog."

34

"How?"

"She has a GPS tag on her collar. Maybe you should get one for the kid?"

I was about to retort that Alfie wasn't an animal when I realised a GPS tag actually wouldn't be a bad idea, especially if it stopped me from having a coronary.

"Ah, fuck," Chip muttered.

"What? What is it?"

Chip didn't answer my panicked question, but I heard the muffled sound of running. A yell. Barking. A loud splash. The splash came from the other side of the wall—the ten-foot-high wall—and it's amazing what adrenaline can do to the body. I practically ran up the nearest tree, slithered along a sturdy branch, and belly-flopped onto the brickwork.

Oh hell! Alfie was in the bloody swimming pool, splashing around in the water with the dog, a giant wolflike thing who thought it was a great game and kept trying to grab his arms. But Alfie was panicking. His screams sounded anything but joyous. I tried to jump off the wall, bracing for impact, but found myself dangling in midair when my leather belt caught on a metal bracket halfway down. All I could do was swing and shriek.

"Alfie!"

My heart thudded against my ribcage as a floppy-haired man in sweatpants and a white T-shirt sprinted from the house and dove into the deep end with no hesitation whatsoever. A moment later, Alfie was sitting on the edge of the pool while the dog paddled to the far end and clambered up the steps.

Alfie was okay.

Alfie was okay.

My phone rang, and I managed to get it out of my back pocket, but my hands were shaking so much that I dropped it. I swung helplessly as it bounced off a stone plant pot and came to rest with a shattered screen. Dammit. I blinked back tears as I focused on trying to get myself unhooked, but I couldn't reach the top of the wall to pull myself up, and my weight kept the belt buckle pulled tight.

"Easy, Janie."

Chip wrapped his arms around my legs and lifted me high enough to unhook the belt, then lowered me gently to the ground.

"You're okay. Everything's okay."

But everything wasn't okay. When I looked up, I realised why his voice had seemed familiar. Why I'd felt so weird around this place. Why even now, my thighs were clenching from being so close to this stranger who wasn't actually a stranger.

Eyes.

Or rather, Eye, because now he was wearing a patch over the right one. Before I could stop myself, I lifted a hand, but he reacted quicker than I'd ever seen a man move and blocked my slap with his forearm.

"You bastard!"

He looked more worn around the edges—longer hair, creases in his forehead, and scarred skin by the eye with the patch. But his body hadn't changed much. Under the wet T-shirt that clung to his pecs, he was as chiselled as I remembered. Muscled perfection.

And still a massive dick.

Man, the dick. I glanced down before I could help myself, and his grey sweatpants were soaking too.

Nope, he's absolutely a jerk.

Alfie sidled up to us with the dog, dripping, and I spotted a worm crawling out of his trouser pocket. *Heaven help me.* And his cast was wet. Would it dry out, or did we need to go back to the hospital?

"Mum said a bad word."

"Sometimes that's necessary," Eyes told him.

"Do not encourage my son to swear. Alfie, we're leaving."

"Janie..."

"You didn't want to speak to me thirteen years ago? Well, I don't want to speak to you now. You can fix your own damn door."

Alfie's eyes widened. "That's two bad words. What happened to your face, mister?"

Please, ground, swallow me up.

"We're leaving *right now.*"

The worm plopped onto the gravel, and I flounced off with Alfie, although my dramatic exit was somewhat scuppered when I realised I had no idea where I was going.

"How did you get in here?" I whispered.

Alfie shrugged.

Eyes was smirking, the giant prick. He nodded towards the door in the wall.

"That's the fastest way out. Bolt's on the inside."

I gave him the finger over my shoulder as I marched away, which Alfie thankfully missed because he was too busy pointing at a beehive by the far wall. No, we weren't going to check out the bees. With my current run of luck, they'd sting me into a swollen blob and I'd have to spend another eight hours in A&E.

Harry was standing on the front steps when Alfie squelched his way around the corner ahead of me.

"I went swimming!" he gleefully told his big brother. "I made a massive splash. And even though I definitely wasn't drowning, a giant rescued me and Mum tried to punch him."

Was it wrong to wish I'd had a girl? A girl wouldn't have cannonballed into the swimming pool, and she definitely wouldn't have cannonballed into the swimming pool with worms on board.

"Alfie, stand on the lawn and empty your pockets. Harry, pick up whatever painting stuff is ours and bring it with us."

"I don't have anything in—" Alfie started.

"All of it."

Grudgingly, he evicted another worm, three snails, and a motley crew of woodlice.

"Does this mean I don't have to do the gloss paint?" Harry asked.

"You can watch TV for the rest of the day."

"Sweet."

We had to walk three-quarters of the way home. That was how long it took for Alfie to dry out enough to get on the bus. Chip, Eyes, whatever he was calling himself this week tried to ring me, and I took great pleasure in blocking his number. Had he known it was me when we first spoke? Was that why he'd given me a false name? *Chip?* Pah. Obviously, Eyes was a nickname too, but— What did I care anyway? He was out of my life. Again. He could hang out on his fancy estate at one end of Engleby while I slummed it with the mortals at the other.

We. Were. Done.

Seven

The first bouquet of flowers arrived on Monday morning when the boys were at school.

Roses, carnations, snapdragons, and alstroemerias in a glass vase, together with a card that said simply *I'm Sorry*.

I threw the whole lot in the bin.

Then stewed for half an hour.

Then retrieved the bouquet and put it in the dreary living room because nobody had ever bought me flowers before, and they really were quite pretty. It wasn't as if Eyes would know I'd kept them. He could just imagine I'd tossed them out the window and stomped their wilted remains into the mud.

And I deserved the flowers.

He *should* be sorry.

Sorry for what he'd done, and sorry for stirring up bad memories.

I'd first met Eyes in the village shop a couple of days before *that* night. Our hands had brushed when we both reached for the last iceberg lettuce at the same time, and he told me I should take it. Then he'd held the door open as I struggled out with two heavy bags.

"Want me to carry those for you?" he asked. "Which car is yours?"

"I'm walking."

He frowned, which was a habit of his, judging by the lines I'd seen on his forehead yesterday.

"I'd offer you a lift, but I'd also advise you against accepting rides from strange men, which leaves me in something of a quandary. Want me to call you a cab?"

"I'm fine, honestly." Then, "Are you admitting you're strange?"

Finally, he smiled, and that flipped him from merely handsome to devastating. "A little."

Then he'd sauntered off to his car—a BMW, I remembered—and driven out of my life.

Or so I'd thought.

On a warm August evening two days later, I'd ventured out to the Hand and Flowers to show my face at Veronica Delven's eighteenth birthday bash. I didn't much like Veronica, but my mum worked in the office at the local golf club with Veronica's mum, so I had to make an appearance to keep the peace. I'd only been there for ten minutes when Eyes walked in. And he'd looked...unhappy.

"Still lamenting the lack of lettuce?" I asked.

"What?" Then recognition flickered in his eyes. "No lettuce tonight." He nodded towards the bar. "What can I get you?"

"So I shouldn't accept a lift from a strange man, but it's okay to take a drink?"

"As long as you watch the bartender pour it, and you don't let it out of your sight."

One drink turned into two, and as the pub became

busier and I grew tipsy, I found myself nestled on his lap. Warmth from his broad chest seeped into me, and my pre-cellulite ass felt quite at home on his muscular thighs. Chairs were so overrated. The way his arm snaked around my waist said "mine," and the handful of guys who tried approaching us backed hurriedly away when they caught sight of Eyes's fierce expression. I kind of liked that. Feeling wanted, I mean. In those days, I'd had the time to make an effort with my appearance, and people always told me I was pretty. I thought my nose was a bit big and my teeth were crooked, but I didn't look terrible.

Two drinks turned into three, and a perch at the busy bar turned into a cosy bench seat in the quietest corner we could find. And we talked. Or rather, *I* talked. In hindsight, I realised Eyes had asked me an awful lot of questions about myself without giving much away in return.

He knew my full name was Janie May Taylor, and that I should have been called Jamie, but someone made a typo on my birth certificate and nobody noticed until it was too late. I didn't even know his surname.

He knew I'd graduated from the local comprehensive with four A-levels and no real idea what I wanted to do with the rest of my life, but I'd decided to work in an office for a year or two and save while I figured it out. Maybe I'd go to uni? Maybe I'd travel? The world was my oyster. He'd mentioned having family in London, but beyond that, I had no clue where he came from or what he did for a living.

He knew I dreamed of visiting the Maldives, that I didn't love eating fish, that I enjoyed walking but wasn't a big fan of team sports. He knew I was a Sagittarius, and I had a pet cat named Tiger because he was stripy, and I'd quit driving lessons after backing my dad's car into a wall three days after my seventeenth birthday. I knew he had a sizeable dick. I could feel it against my ass as he whispered in my ear that I was beautiful.

Three drinks turned into four, or five, or six. Daniel Menzies puked on the dance floor, and after that, people began to drift off home, or possibly to a nightclub in town. Eyes wanted to call me a cab, but I told him I'd be fine walking, that I'd done it a hundred times and knew the way. He'd insisted he was coming with me to make sure I stayed safe.

I wasn't entirely certain how we'd ended up at the nature reserve. Maybe I'd wanted to show him the moonlight on the lake, or perhaps I just wasn't ready to say goodbye. Kisses turned into more, and he'd taken my virginity on the dusty floor of the birdwatcher's hide. *Taken.* That made it sound as if he stole it, but make no mistake, it was freely given. It was only what came afterwards that left me with regrets.

The metaphorical punch that hit me from left field.

Eyes had returned to London, a commitment he couldn't miss, he said. He'd texted me a hundred times in the days that followed, called me on Sunday, Monday, and Tuesday too. Then on Wednesday, he went quiet.

My "are you okay?" message stayed unread for hours before he delivered the death blow.

EYES

This isn't how I wanted to end things, Janie, but I don't have a choice. It's nothing you've done. This is all on me. Be happy, and I'll never forget you.

That was it. Poof. Gone. Until Harry threw paint over the door at Twilight's End, and the world's biggest, most spectacular dick came back into my life.

He'd never forget me? What a crock of shit. He

probably hadn't given me another thought after he sent that text, not until Harry ruined his porch, anyway.

I sighed as I added water to the vase. This time, the decision on whether to talk was mine, and Eyes could go fuck himself.

Eight

More flowers arrived on Tuesday. And Wednesday, and Thursday, and Friday. I was running out of places to put them all, and Alfie had started sniffling. There was a nasty cold going around at school, which was most likely the reason, but what if he was allergic to pollen? Was there a test for that?

At least I wouldn't have to worry about it today. Steven picked the boys up every other weekend, usually on a Friday evening but sometimes on a Saturday morning if he had some vitally important social event he couldn't miss, and they wouldn't be back until Sunday.

"I thought you were getting this fixed," he said, poking the rotten window frame beside the door with his house key while he waited for Harry to find his Nintendo charger.

"Oh, sure, money just grows on trees. If you paid your child support, I could fix things faster."

"My solicitor needs to check something on the forms."

Same old, same old. "If he's taking that long, you should find a better solicitor."

As always, Steven ignored that suggestion. "Harry, you ready?"

Finally, the three of them left, and I knew for a fact that Alfie had three slugs in his pocket, but those were Luisa's problem now.

My problem? The dirt the boys had tracked through the house after a rain shower yesterday.

I thought the florist would be closed on Saturday, that I might get some respite, but the doorbell rang just after nine o'clock, and when I peered through the peephole with a mop in my hand, the biggest bunch of roses I'd ever seen filled the view.

For crying out loud.

I yanked the door open. "Look, my whole house is filled with flowers. Next time you get a delivery for this address, could you just take them to the hospital instead? Or the old folks' home? Or the cemetery?"

The delivery guy lowered the flowers, and I realised that the sneaky sod had pulled a bait-and-switch.

"You'd rather have chocolates?" Eyes asked.

"Which part of 'I don't want to speak to you' did you not understand?"

"I need to apologise."

"You already did that in writing. Five times." I folded my arms and fought back tears. "Just leave me alone."

"I tried that. Why do you think I stayed in my house last weekend? But now you know I'm around, and I want to clear the air in case we bump into each other again."

"Clear the air? Are you kidding me? I'm choking on lies and half-truths here. You've already screwed me in two different ways, and I don't even know your freaking name. Chip? Seriously?"

"It's a nickname. My friends call me that."

"Well, I'm not your friend. And what about Eyes? Another nickname?"

"No, that's my real name."

"Who calls a child Eyes?"

"My parents? It's short for Eisen."

"Eisen?"

"E-I-S-E-N. Eis for short. Wait, how did you think it was spelled?"

"That doesn't matter. What matters is that you're a lying bastard."

"You thought it was E-Y-E-S?" He pointed at his own face, then grimaced. "Like the body part?"

"Well, you have very striking eyes. Eye." I smacked my own forehead. "Sorry. Sorry for being insensitive, and sorry for whatever happened to...you know."

"You have nothing to apologise for. The blame lies squarely with me. Will you let me explain? Please?"

Should I? If I kicked his oh-so-fine backside off my property, a broken part of me would always wonder why he'd done what he did. Why he'd led me on and then dumped me by text. Didn't I deserve closure?

"Janie?"

"If I say yes, do you promise to leave straight after?"

"Unless you want me to stay."

"There's no chance of that." I pulled the door closed behind me and put my hands on my hips. No way was I inviting him in. "Fine. Explain."

Now it was his turn to hesitate. "Fuck, I don't even know where to start."

"How about answering a simple question: why did you screw me in a birdwatcher's hide, sweet-talk me over the phone for three days, and then disappear? What did I do wrong? You owe me that much."

"You did nothing wrong. The short answer is that I went to prison."

Prison?

Prison?

Oh, hell. And now this criminal was on my doorstep. The hedge was overgrown, and the road outside was quiet. If he decided to murder me, would anyone even hear me scream? Eis was huge, six feet of solid muscle, and if he tried to subdue me, I wouldn't stand a chance. All I had to defend myself was a freaking mop.

"Leave. Just leave." I tried to sound strong, but I couldn't keep the tremor out of my voice. "Get the hell away from me."

Eis took two steps back, but his gaze stayed focused on my face. "Don't look at me that way, Janie. I'm not going to hurt you. I'd never hurt you."

"I can't do this."

"Please, just hear me out."

I fumbled my phone out of my pocket and typed in 999. My thumb hovered over the "call" button.

"If you take one step farther forward, I'm calling the police."

"Fair enough." He blew out a long breath. "That's fair enough. So... My lawyer thought I'd end up with community service. And then I figured I'd find a way to tell you what happened, and maybe things would be okay. But the cops dressed it up as assault with a deadly weapon, and I got four years, two with parole."

"A weapon?" Now *I* took a step back, only for the door to get in my way. "What kind of weapon?"

"My fist."

"But...but that's not a weapon."

"Apparently when you're a pro fighter and you're assigned the wrong judge, it is." He sighed. "The motherfucker who raped my sister was talking shit to her, so I broke his jaw and a couple of ribs. I'm not sorry."

There was so much to unpack in that. Rape? Broken ribs? He'd never even told me that he had a sister.

"I...I don't know what to say."

"Then just listen. Sending that 'it's not you, it's me' text was the last thing I did before a copper took my phone, and I only had a few seconds to decide what to say. I got it wrong, and then I had no way to fix things. I'm sorry for that. I'll always be sorry. My head was fucked, and I thought letting you go was the best option. I mean, would you have waited two years for me? We'd known each other for less than a week. Later, I wished I'd sent Edie to talk with you instead, but by then, it was too late."

"Who's Edie?"

"My little sister. I made a mess of everything, and I get that. After I was released, I tried to find you, but I heard you were married with a kid, so I stayed away. Janie, I just want you to be happy, but now I look at you and I see that you're not."

The tears came, but Eis stayed where he was, a rock in a stormy sea. He didn't move forward an inch.

And he was right. This *was* a mess.

Despite the gulf between us, despite the heartache he'd caused, I still felt that crazy pull, the invisible current that had first zapped me when he handed me a lettuce.

"He cheated on me," I whispered, meaning Steven. "With my boss."

"Then he's a fucking idiot."

"I thought he was the safe option. The opposite of you."

"You think I'm dangerous?"

"Well, you did tear my heart in two. You hurt me, Eis. You really hurt me. I can't just forget about that."

He managed a lopsided smile. "At the moment, I'd settle

for you not crossing the road when you see me coming. And yeah, I'm handy with my fists, but I swear I'll never lay a finger on you."

I motioned towards his eye. "Was that another fight?"

He shook his head. "A colleague was having trouble with an ex, so I offered to walk her to her car one night. The fucker was hiding between two vehicles, and he threw acid at her."

I couldn't hold back my gasp. "It hit you too?"

"I saw him a second before she did and shoved her down, but I couldn't get out of the way fast enough. That..." Eis took a deep breath. "That really screwed with my head. I'd always felt invincible, you know? Physically, anyway. Then suddenly, I was sedated in the ICU having one surgery after another, and everything was out of my control. I couldn't even use the fucking bathroom on my own. And when I came out, that was worse. I had to adjust to a whole new life. Janie, don't look at me that way."

"What way?"

"With pity. I preferred the anger."

"Sorry. I'm sorry. I need to think about this, okay? I just need some space."

"Okay."

"You said you'd leave."

"And I will. About the chocolates...?"

My head screamed *no, no, no,* but my heart overruled the same way it had thirteen years ago. This man had a way of making me stupid. Okay, stupider. I'd already proven with Steven that my judgment was sorely lacking.

"Maybe the occasional box would be all right."

Nine

That night, I dreamed of Eisen. The boy he'd been mixed with the man he'd become. The muscles, the beautiful sapphire eyes, the cocoon of safety he'd wrapped me in that night in the Hand and Flowers. He'd said he once felt invincible, and I understood why because when I was with him, I'd felt it too.

But could I believe his words? Could I ever trust him again?

When I failed to get back to sleep, I consulted Google. Eisen was an unusual name, and maybe the acid attack had been reported online? Those sorts of events were still rare enough that they might get a mention on local news.

That was when I found out who Eisen really was.

What he'd kept from me all those years ago, and what he'd still skated around yesterday. Once I had his surname, the internet gave up his secrets, hundreds of articles and pictures and interviews.

Things I'd never have found unless I knew where to look.

I didn't watch the news much—when did I ever get the time?—and I certainly didn't follow the world of MMA.

The headlines told the story. The reporters sensationalised every event, and my heart ached for everything Eis and his family had been through. It certainly put my impending divorce into perspective.

Eisen Kennedy-Renner, aristocrat's son, sentenced to four years for GBH.

Edith Renner defends brother on courthouse steps: Neil Short got what he deserved.

Elizabeth Renner speaks out: my grandson fought for his sister when the legal system failed.

I could certainly understand why Eis had broken Neil Short's jaw. Such a small percentage of rape cases were ever prosecuted, and for the victims, the journey through the legal system was almost as traumatic as the event itself. One of my hairdressing clients had lost a daughter that way—she hadn't been able to live with the memories.

Eisen "Ironman" Renner, disgraced son of Viscount Brigham, wins third WPFL bout.

Ironman Renner opens gym in Hammersmith - local women encouraged to sign up for free self-defence classes.

Ironman defeats Maxim Chechkov in fifth round to take world title.

Ironman's Four Rings fitness empire goes from strength to strength.

Photo after photo showed Eis in a cage, beating the living daylights out of his opponents. There was even video. In one tiny respect, the judge in his trial had been right—his hands were lethal weapons. Eisen had a reputation for defending what was his, and more than once, he'd lashed out at reporters—verbally—when they tried to talk about his sister. Meanwhile, I'd been stuck with Steven, who hadn't said a word when one of his colleagues called me "a bit grumpy" at his work Christmas party.

Elizabeth Renner lobbies for Edie's Law: No woman should be without a voice.

World champ rushed to hospital after attack in car park.

Neil Short, defendant in Renner civil case, jailed after new victim fights back.

Elizabeth Renner, businesswoman and women's rights powerhouse, dies in hospital after a short illness.

I recognised Elizabeth Renner from one of the photos. When I was eight or nine, she'd had her driver park beside the village green, hobbled over to Marissa and me, and told us to stop throwing rocks in the duck pond. We'd thought the ripples were pretty; it hadn't occurred to us that we might scare the creatures that lived there.

It seemed that Eisen had inherited more than Twilight's End from his grandma—he'd also gotten her protective streak. Maybe I couldn't forget what he'd done, but could I forgive?

In between listening to the rain drip, drip, drip through the roof and emptying buckets, I unblocked Eis's number.

ME

> Perhaps someday if you're passing, you could drop in for coffee?

The sound of a car engine woke me, and I groaned. I needed to replace the front gate so people didn't keep using the driveway to turn around. The original gate had fallen off its hinges when I tried to close it, and now it was lying where it had fallen, waiting for me to find the spoons to do something about it.

Then someone knocked on the door, and I groaned harder. For once in my life, couldn't I have a lie-in? If a tourist was lost, they could phone a friend. Or had I forgotten an appointment? Maybe the plumber had come early... No, it was a Sunday. The plumber wouldn't come on a Sunday, and he wasn't due for another month anyway.

I rolled out of bed and stumbled down the stairs. One day, I'd move into the bedroom at the front of the house, but for now, I was in the box room at the back where the rain didn't get in. Until I moved into Marigold Lodge, I hadn't appreciated basic comforts like a structurally sound roof enough.

And I also hadn't fully understood what it would mean to have a man like Eisen Renner in my life. Today, he wasn't hiding behind flowers. He just had a hoodie pulled low over his face.

I yanked the door open. "What are you doing here?"

"You said to drop in for coffee if I was passing."

"Oh, and you just happened to be passing first thing this morning?"

"Yeah."

"Really?"

"I went out to get you breakfast, and on the way back, I was passing."

"For goodness' sake. It's..." I checked my wrist, then remembered my watch was on the bedside table.

"It's nearly ten o'clock," he supplied.

Oh. "Yes, well, I was up half the night, uh..." I could hardly tell him I'd been picking apart his life on the internet, could I? "...uh, doing stuff."

"You mean you were googling me?"

How did he know?

"Why on earth would you think that?"

53

"Because there are only two reasons you would have texted me at four thirty a.m."

"Oh yeah? What's the second one?"

"Last weekend, you weren't as subtle as you thought you were when you checked out my junk." Dammit! "I brought coffee as well. One black, one with all the froth and syrup and shit. Drink whichever you want, and I'll have the other."

"Eis, I'm still in my pyjamas."

"You can take them off if you want. I don't mind."

I'd given him the tiniest of openings, and now he was kicking his way through my defences, Jackie Chan style. *Kapow.* I could probably still slam the door if I put my mind to it, but did I want to? Eis had haunted my dreams for years, and even though I'd wanted to hate him, deep down, I'd always hoped he had a good reason for doing what he did. That one night together, he'd looked after me. Been so freaking gentle. I'd confessed it was my first time, and his protective streak had been out in full force. He'd even made me pee in a bush afterwards so I didn't get a UTI, which was a little embarrassing but also weirdly thoughtful, and then he'd dressed me tenderly and let me use his chest as a pillow while we watched the stars. Losing my virginity on a dirt floor in a nature reserve—it should have been a bit icky, but he'd made it almost romantic.

My first time with Steven, I'd gone to pee afterwards and found him snoring in bed when I got back. He didn't even take off his socks.

As Eis walked past me, I poked him in the chest.

"If you ever hurt me again, I'll chop off your balls while you sleep."

"If I ever hurt you again, I'll hand you the knife."

Ten

⟨⟨⟩⟩

"So, why do your friends call you Chip?"

I'd changed into leggings and a slouchy sweater, and now we were sitting in the kitchen with the scarred oak table the previous owner had left behind between us. I'd also combed my hair. Honestly, I was surprised Eis hadn't left when he saw the bird's nest on my head this morning, but he was still here, and he'd even wedged a fresh piece of cardboard under the wobbly table leg.

"You know I fought MMA?"

I nodded.

"Most fighters have a ring name."

"You were Ironman."

"Right. Because Eisen means 'iron' in German. But for my first fight, one of my buddies was commentating, and he thought it would be funny to introduce me as Raging Chipmunk."

I nearly spat a mouthful of croissant across the table, which would have been a shame because they were the good ones from the fancy bakery in the next town.

"Raging Chipmunk?" I pretended to study him. "Yes, I can see it."

He threw a piece of croissant at me.

"Perhaps you could try a movie career?" I suggested. "*Crouching Hamster, Hidden Pussycat*?"

He picked up both of our knives and whirled them like tiny swords. "Chipmunks have rules too."

"That movie had some great lines."

Eis laughed. "You still watch a lot of movies?"

"I love movies and books. Anything to escape from the real world."

He reached across the table to cup my cheek. It was the first time he'd touched me since he'd hoisted me skywards in his walled garden, and I leaned into him. I couldn't help it.

"Maybe someday, you'll build a world you don't want to escape from."

My emotions were there, bubbling so treacherously close to the surface, and I blinked back tears again.

"That's just a pipe dream."

Quite literally.

"Tell me what you need, Janie."

"What I need?"

"Right now, what do you need to make your life easier?"

My turn to laugh. "A plumber."

"A plumber?"

"I already paid a small fortune to one cowboy who made everything worse, so now I'm waiting for the guy that everyone says is good, but he has a waiting list longer than *War and Peace*. Ditto for the roofing chap."

"What's wrong with the plumbing?"

"What isn't wrong with it? Joints leak, pipes leak, the shower that doesn't leak needs a new pump, and the central heating doesn't work."

"Want me to take a look?"

56

"Since when did you go to plumbing school?"

"Since I was in prison and there were a bunch of classes we could take. I can weave a decent basket too."

"I'm not even sure whether you're joking or not."

"Give me cane and raffia, and we'll find out." He kissed my palm. He *kissed my freaking palm.* "And I'm serious about the plumbing. I've done a bunch of work at the cottage since I moved in as well."

"The cottage?"

"Twilight's End."

"Twilight's End is *not* a cottage. And I'm really sorry about your grandma."

"Me too. She was a tough old bird. We all thought she'd be around forever, but her gin habit finally caught up."

"You got along well, huh? Were you visiting with her when we first met?"

"I came to drown my sorrows before the trial. But she locked the liquor away, so I went to the Hand and Flowers, and that was when I met you again. Funny how fate works, isn't it? The court case brought us together, and then it forced us apart."

"And now you're here."

"Now I'm here."

There was a long silence as our gazes locked, and we both smiled at the same time. Maybe later, much later, I'd raise a glass to Grandma Renner.

Eis dug through my meagre toolbox and tutted a bit, then poked around the rest of Marigold Lodge. His verdict?

"You're right; the plumbing's fucked."

"Super. Maybe I could just knock the house down and start again? At least a tent would be waterproof."

"I've written a list of the stuff we need. You'll have to get an engineer for the boiler, but I can help with the rest."

I didn't want his help. No, actually, that wasn't quite right. I didn't want to *need* his help. But pride was a luxury I could no longer afford, along with branded groceries and the electricity bill.

"The big hardware store has plumbing stuff, I think. I mean, there are pipes and joints and tubes of sealant."

"I'll get everything delivered this week."

"Here?"

"No point in getting it delivered to my place."

"Uh, okay? I have some clients booked in, but if I know when the delivery might come..."

"Clients?"

"At Cutting Edge. I work as a hairdresser, but only during school hours. Mostly the older clientele because they're retired. I was supposed to be doing Mavis Butterfield's perm today, but her brother's in the hospital, and— You don't really need to know any of that."

"Right."

"What did you think I was doing all day?"

A shrug. "Being a mother?"

"That's not a job."

"Yeah, it is."

"Okay, it's not a job that pays money. Did your mum stay at home all day?"

"No, but we had a nanny."

Eis and me, we came from different worlds. His family had staff. He lived in a mansion-slash-castle and owned a thriving business. I lived hand to mouth and prayed we had a mild winter because the boys and I would freeze otherwise.

"Well, I've got to work, Eis. I'm really lucky because my

sister won the lottery and bought this place for me to live in rent-free, but we need to eat."

He sucked in a breath. "We'll go to the hardware store today."

"But you don't want to." I'd have to be blind to miss the tension in his shoulders and the way his fists clenched at his sides. He hated the idea. But why? Then I realised. I realised that in all my googling, I'd never found anything recent. His online story stopped with the incident in the car park. He'd been carted off in an ambulance, and after that, he'd disappeared from public life. And at Twilight's End, he'd been fine with my anger but not with my pity. "You worry about people looking at you?"

"Either they stare, or they do that thing where they pretend to be engrossed in something else and keep glancing in my direction. Strangers can't look me in the eye anymore, and I know what they're thinking—*poor dumb fuck, what happened to him?* Sometimes I want to wear a sign: *it was acid, I know it's ugly.*" He gave the heaviest sigh. "It used to be much worse. Right after it happened, my skin was red and angry, and Edie keeps telling me it looks okay now, but I'd still rather stay at home. Fuck," he spat. "Now who's having the pity party?"

"Edie's right."

"I wish I was still the man you met thirteen years ago."

"You *are* the man I met thirteen years ago. Just with slightly better communication skills, I hope."

"But I look different."

"And you think I don't? Eis, I've had two babies. I hate taking the boys to the pool because I don't have a bikini body anymore, and my boobs need a push-up bra to look anything close to perky. You're sitting there looking as if you want to eat me alive, and I'm sitting here thinking that you'd better be fond of rice pudding because that's what my cellulite looks like. And then there's my stretch—"

"Enough."

Eis shoved his chair back and stalked angrily around the table. Before I could properly process, I was in his arms, pressed tight against his hard chest with his day-old stubble tickling my forehead.

"Don't talk shit about yourself, Janie. You're beautiful."

"You really think that?"

"It's the truth."

"Then why won't you believe you're beautiful too?"

We clung to each other for an age. Just stood there in the kitchen, silently finding our way back to each other, our embrace saying more than words ever could. At some point, I started crying. Finally, Eis loosened his grip and kissed my hair.

"Let's go out."

"This is going to be messy."

He knew I wasn't talking about the shopping trip. "It is."

"We're going to fight a lot."

"The make-up sex will be spectacular."

"Are you sure?"

"Positive."

I'd never had make-up sex with Steven. We never really used to argue. I'd always thought that meant we were compatible, but standing there with six feet of cocky red-blooded male in front of me, I realised the truth. I'd never fought with Steven because I'd never been bothered enough to care. If he worked late, so what? I'd just read a book. If he said he was too tired for sex, who cared? I had a vibrator hidden in the bathroom cabinet, and it did a better job than him anyway. Most of our tiffs had been about the boys.

About Steven letting them down when they needed him most.

Eleven years ago, I'd found myself pregnant and done what I thought was the right thing at the time.

Which turned out to be the wrong thing.

Now I was at the top of a roller coaster, waiting for the ride to start. For the twists, the turns, the exhilaration. The safety bar was probably faulty, but I couldn't get off, even if I wanted to.

"Is it okay to be a little bit scared?" I asked.

"I'm fucking terrified. Terrified of screwing this up, terrified of losing you again."

"Can we take things slowly?"

"How slowly?"

"No side trips to the nature reserve today."

Eis chuckled into my hair. "It's raining anyway."

"Be serious."

"Fine, we'll take things slowly, but understand this. I'm your past, Janie, but I'm also your future. Don't think for one second that I'm not."

A few months ago, Marissa had told me that the best thing about being with Liam was having someone who was hers. An ally who fought in her corner, who loved her to the moon and back, and who was always there for her, no matter what. At the time, I'd been baffled by her words because the best thing about being with Steven was that he paid half the rent and occasionally picked up a chippy tea on his way home from work.

But now I understood.

I understood that Eisen Renner was going to shake my world to its very core, and then we were going to build something new from the rubble.

And we'd start our journey at the hardware store.

Eleven

E is held my hand in a death grip as we walked into Hardware HQ. Years ago, the one word I'd have used to describe him was "confident," and it hurt my heart that a jealous nutcase had stolen that from him. The acid attacker was in jail now. According to the news reports, Eis had felled him with a single punch before the police arrived.

The female victim, a petite blonde named Madison, had worked at one of his gyms, a personal trainer and occasional ring girl who'd met her assailant through a dating app and been out with him only a handful of times before coming to the conclusion he was bad news. Then he'd stalked her for months, leaving her scared to live in her own home.

Eis had been at the gym for a routine visit when he'd done the gentlemanly thing and offered to see her safely to her vehicle, and he paid the price for his kindness. Madison still had her sight, but she'd lost most of an ear to the acid.

Rather than hiding away as Eis had done, she'd been speaking out about the ordeal, and in recent months, she'd started a podcast to talk about her recovery. It was on my "to be listened to" list. The subject matter was grim, but I desperately wanted to understand what Eis was going through.

While I overthought everything, he loaded the trolley with pipes and widgets and gubbins and a whole bunch of other stuff. Me? I watched people watching him. And they did watch him. Everyone looked. His broad shoulders, the graceful way he moved, his assets in those freaking sweatpants... They all drew people's attention. And with his head down and his hood pulled forward, he only became more mysterious. People couldn't keep their eyes off him. A woman my age bumped her trolley into ours and apologised profusely.

"So sorry, I was just a little distracted."

"It's fine."

But it wasn't fine. Every time a girl checked out his backside, I wanted to poke her in the eye with a screwdriver. Was that normal?

"We're done," he said.

And then we had our first argument.

If I'd thought about things ahead of time, it was inevitable, really. We reached the checkout, and I got out my credit card. Then Eis got out his credit card, which was black and shiny and had his fancy name. *E Kennedy-Renner.*

"This is my stuff," I told him. "I'm paying."

"No."

"What?"

"No."

I just stared at him. This wasn't a situation I'd experienced before. Whenever it came to paying, Steven conveniently wandered off to look at something on the other side of the shop.

"You can't buy pipes for my house. You're already providing the labour."

He flashed me the dirtiest smile. "I'm a full-service kind of guy."

"I know that, but... Wait, wait, I *don't* know that." Everyone in the queue was gawping. The checkout lady's gaze was ping-ponging between us in rapt fascination. "Honestly."

"You can service my pipes any time, darlin'," a woman called from behind us, but Eis's attention was focused on me.

"When I bought all the drinks in the Hand and Flowers, you didn't complain."

"That was different. That was a date, sort of."

"We can go and make out by the ballcocks if it would help you to feel better."

"The ballcocks? Is that a plumbing thing? Or are you being filthy again?"

"Yes."

"Yes to which one?"

"Both."

I closed my eyes and took a calming breath. This man was impossible. Frustrating, demanding, bossy. Hot. So, so hot.

He leaned in closer. "I forgot to look for the nipples."

"Okay. Okay! You win. Fine, pay for the damn stuff."

There was a round of applause as he handed over his credit card, and I wasn't even sure who folks were clapping for. Nothing would ever be easy with Eisen Renner, but for the first time in years, I felt alive. Energised.

Maybe even happy.

"Does that count as a fight?" he asked as we headed back to his SUV, and I didn't miss the note of hope in his voice.

"We're taking things slow, remember? No make-up sex today."

"Will you yell at me if I buy you dinner?"

"Probably."

"Indian? Chinese? Italian?" he asked. "Or sushi?"

Eis didn't get that body from curry and carbs. "Sushi's your favourite?"

He nodded.

"Then we'll have sushi."

We actually did go to the nature reserve—Primrose needed a walk—but there were far too many people around for us to get up to any funny business, much to Eis's disappointment. Primrose had been Elizabeth Renner's service dog, I found out, which was why she knew how to open doors. Plus she could turn lights on and off and pick up objects if you dropped them. When we got back, Eis gave me a proper tour of Twilight's End and its rabbit warren of rooms. It turned out he didn't own the house, not completely. The estate belonged to Edie too, and he owned half of the house in Kensington where she spent most of her time. It was clear from the way he spoke that he adored his little sister.

Eis had converted a barn beside the walled garden into a gym, complete with a fight cage, but he hadn't touched the old stables because Edie loved horses, and they figured that if either of them ever had a little girl who wanted a pony, it would need somewhere to live. There was the pool, a sauna, a steam room, a hot tub, a games room, a movie theatre... I began to see why Eis never left the place.

Dinner was delivered, and I thought we'd eat in the kitchen or the dining room or maybe the orangery, but instead, he led me to the fanciest of the three staircases.

"How long have we got?" he asked.

"At least two hours."

Steven had taken Harry to watch a football match, but because he only had two tickets, he'd left Alfie behind with Luisa. Which was apparently okay because Alfie "doesn't really get football anyway."

It wasn't okay.

Luisa's idea of childcare was to give the boys snacks and sit them in front of the TV, or worse, let them loose with craft materials. Earlier in the year, she'd sent Alfie home with a Lego brick superglued to his forehead. And the snacks were always the unhealthy, sugary kind, which meant both boys would be bouncing off the walls until the early hours and I'd get no sleep again.

But that was a problem for later.

Right now, I faced a much bigger challenge.

I will not lose my clothes, I will not lose my clothes, I will not lose my clothes.

You have to understand, waxing hadn't been high on my list of priorities these past few months, and the area between my legs resembled an overgrown wasteland. I needed to go on a crash diet, do three hundred crunches a day, and buy every cellulite-busting cream on the market in the hope that one of them worked.

Eis got to the top of the main staircase and opened a door we'd walked past earlier. I'd assumed it was a closet, but inside, a narrow spiral staircase wound upwards to a cosy room that contained a couch, a coffee table, and a bookcase. Half a dozen steps at one end led to a funny little platform under a dome.

"This was my grandfather's observatory." Eis flipped a switch on the wall, and the whole ceiling rolled back to reveal the sparkling sky above. "His favourite room in the house, and mine too. This might be the last night this year that it's warm enough to open the roof."

"It's...it's beautiful." And so unexpected. My favourite

room was the library with its floor-to-ceiling shelves and rolling ladders, but this came a close second.

"I wanted to bring you here the night we ended up at the nature reserve, but Grandma was holding a bridge party, and I thought we'd have more time." He brought the back of my hand to his lips. "I thought we'd have so much more time."

We ate sushi under the stars, and we talked. Eis kept his promise not to rush things and instead pointed out the different constellations as we lay on the sofa, my head nestled against his shoulder. It reminded me of our first night together, just without the sex or the peeing-in-a-bush parts.

"This is the first evening in I-can't-remember-how-long that I've taken an hour to do nothing," I confessed. "It's weird."

"That's a feeling I understand. Fifteen months ago, I never had a moment to myself, and then suddenly I had all the time in the world."

"I'm so sorry."

"I realise now that my old life wasn't the one I wanted, but that didn't make losing it easy."

"That's a feeling *I* understand. I hadn't been happy for a long time, but the idea of starting again from nothing was terrifying."

"What do you miss from your old life?"

Nobody had ever asked me that before. "I guess...I guess the security. Although we were living in a house of cards, I know that now. Steven dealt with the finances, and it was a mess. Probably still is a mess. My solicitor helped me to take my name off all the joint stuff, but my credit rating is shot to pieces." I sighed. "So, what does that leave? Social status, maybe. People look at you differently when you're a wife. As if it's something to aspire to."

"We're not so different, you and me."

"Oh, please. Your roof is actually designed to be open to the elements."

Eis laughed and rolled onto his side to face me. "People looked at me differently when I was a champion compared to when I was a victim."

"You still are a champion. Nobody can take that away from you."

He shrugged one shoulder. "Big pieces of my life vanished overnight. My ex came to visit me in the hospital the day after it happened. Once. She came once, and after she left, she called Edie and told her that 'this wasn't what I signed up for.'"

"She broke up with you via your sister?"

"Makes sending a text message seem classy, huh?"

I narrowed my eyes at him. "Don't go there."

"It was worth a try."

"You couldn't continue with your career?"

"Not with the amount of peripheral vision I have at the moment. I need to see a move coming and have time to react. Mostly, I'm watching the guy's waist, but I also need to be aware of the cage, the ref, his hands..."

"I hate that you lost something you love."

Eis brushed my hair away from my face. "When I got out of prison, I was so fucking angry. Every time I went into the cage, I imagined I was facing Neil Short. You know who he is?"

"The man who forced himself on your sister?"

"Yeah, but he was no man. He was scum. I let that anger fuel me, and that's why I won every fight. He'd taken two years of my life, but worst of all, he'd taken you."

There was so much unbearable agony in Eis's voice that my heart broke all over again. If I ever met Neil Short, I'd be at risk of doing jail time too.

"But I'm here now. And Neil Short is in prison, isn't he?"

Eis nodded. "Every single one of my gyms offers free self-defence courses for women and free safety classes for kids. Stranger danger and all that. Short tried his shit on a woman my team had trained, and she put him in the hospital. Plus Edie bankrupted him in the civil trial."

"Good for them."

"None of that makes up for what he did, but I don't feel the all-consuming rage anymore. Maybe I lost my edge?"

"What about the man who threw acid on you? You can't picture his face instead?"

"It doesn't have the same effect. But I made friends on the inside, and he isn't having a good time there. Grandma Elizabeth used to say everything happened for a reason, and I used to tell her that was bullshit, then she used to clip my ear and order me to mind my language. But perhaps she was right?"

"Possibly, but that doesn't excuse Harry from throwing paint at your door."

"I thought my mind was playing tricks when I heard your voice on the phone."

So he *had* recognised me, but he hadn't said anything.

That put another checkmark in the "jerk" column.

"So you gave me a fake name and then hid inside?"

"Would you rather I'd greeted you on the steps with a 'Hey, babe, did you miss me?' If you were still happily married, I wouldn't have interfered."

"I guess I can understand that." I leaned in closer and brushed my lips over his. This man gave me courage I hadn't felt in a long time. "I'm strangely glad you're back in my life, *Chip*."

He touched a finger to his lips. "What happened to taking things slow?"

My turn to shrug.

In a heartbeat, I found myself underneath him, and he returned my kiss with a barely-there one of his own. Electricity charged through me, but when I tried for more, he shook his head.

"Don't start something we can't finish. The boys will be home soon."

A groan escaped. "Are you coming over tomorrow? For the plumbing, I mean. I should buy some dog biscuits for Primrose."

"What time do the boys leave for school?"

"Harry gets the bus at seven thirty, and I walk Alfie to the school in the village at ten past eight. My first appointment is at eleven."

"Mondays, I have a family call at nine, and they never last longer than an hour, so I'll come over after that."

"A family call? Sounds very formal. My family has a WhatsApp group."

"I doubt my cousins use WhatsApp. They'd probably just get their PAs to post sanctimonious reminders about not bringing the family name into disrepute." This time, he kissed my nose. "Text me with your coffee order."

Eis drove me home and waited politely while I walked to the front door. Or at least, I thought that's what he was doing. Safety first, that kind of thing. I was halfway up the path when I heard the car door slam, and then he was on me. One fist tangled in my hair, and his other arm snaked around my waist, lifting me onto my toes so my lips met his. Such soft lips, but the rest of him was hard as granite. Chest, abs, cock... Oh my. His tongue teased the seam of my lips until I gave in and yielded, and then he kissed me so thoroughly that my knees trembled.

Finally, I dredged up every last ounce of willpower and pushed him away.

"Don't start what you can't finish, remember?"

"When are the boys going back to their dad's?"

"The weekend after next."

"Block it out on your schedule. You're mine from the moment they leave."

Twelve

ME

If the offer of coffee is still good, anything with lots of caffeine and sugar would be great.

EISEN

Bad day?

Bad evening, bad night, bad morning. The boys had arrived home two hours late. Harry's coat had disappeared, and Alfie's clothes were covered in felt pen. I'd barely slept because I kept reliving *that* kiss, and at five thirty a.m., Alfie had run into my room crying because his pet spider was missing.

ME

Could be better.

Alfie finally found a spider while I was scraping the remains of the jam-covered toast Harry had dropped off the floor—which may or may not have been the spider he lost—and the batteries in my foil cutter were dead. Annie Crump wanted highlights, which meant I'd need to either buy more batteries or cut the foil manually, and honestly, was anything else going to go wrong today?

Yes.

Yes, of course it was.

When I got back from the school run—why did they call it that when it was more of a sweaty march?—there was a truck parked in my driveway.

"Are you lost?" I asked the man standing beside it.

"Marigold Lodge?"

"Yes, but I didn't order any of...whatever that is."

"It's the scaffolding for your roof."

What?

"I don't understand. I spoke to Kevin last week, and he said I was tenth on the list. That it would be months."

The scaffolding guy shrugged. "Well, now you're first on the list."

"I'm not sure about this."

"You want me to take all the stuff back?"

"I..." Then it hit me. *Eisen*. "Could you give me one moment?"

I dialled his number. The raging chipmunk. The overstepping, uncommunicative chipmunk, more like.

"Do you happen to know why a scaffolding truck just arrived at my house?"

"I thought they were starting tomorrow."

"That's not an answer."

"You need a roof, so I called Kevin and got him to move you up the schedule. I figured that if you had to work tomorrow, I could come over and keep an eye on them."

"How did you get him to move me up the schedule? You didn't threaten to break his legs, did you?"

"Babe, most problems are solved by money, not violence. I offered him drinking vouchers."

"You mean you bribed him?"

"Think of it as a bonus."

"I can't afford a bonus."

"Good thing you're not paying it, then."

"You can't...you can't..."

"It was surprisingly easy. I just went to the ATM, told it how much money I wanted, and dropped the cash through his letter box. In all your googling, did you happen to check out my net worth?"

"No?"

"Well, go and look it up, then tell the man where to park his truck."

Eis hung up. That jerk actually hung up on me, and the scaffolding guy checked his watch.

"I haven't got all day, lady."

"Just one more minute."

I typed "Eisen Renner net worth" into the search bar on my phone. *Holy crap.* Twenty-five million in career winnings, another twenty million in sponsorship deals. Then there was the gym chain he owned, and...oh... *Elizabeth Renner is believed to have bequeathed her entire estate to just two of her four grandchildren, siblings Eisen and Edith, leading to infighting in the family. The value of the estate is an estimated three hundred million pounds, with properties in London, Somerset, Paris, Barbados, and New York.*

I nearly puked.

"Uh, just park the truck wherever. Can I offer you a cup of tea?"

"I'm all right, love."

I walked into the house on autopilot and called Eis again.

"Why didn't you tell me, you absolute twatwaffle?"

"Tell you what?"

"That you're wealthy."

"You didn't get that from the thirty-seven-room mansion?"

"Well, obviously I knew you had some money, but not that you were obscenely filthy stinking rich."

"Does it matter? If I thought you were only after my money, we wouldn't be having this conversation."

"It's just... I guess it's weird."

"The money doesn't define me. It just sits there in the background. If it makes you feel better, I could throw all the cash out of my helicopter."

"You have a helicopter?"

"Technically it's my dad's, but I borrow it sometimes."

Somebody pinch me.

"Throwing cash out of a helicopter seems awfully wasteful. With the way energy bills are going up, wouldn't it make more sense to burn it in the grate?"

Eis just laughed. "I'll see you in a bit."

I sat down hard on the stairs. How was I meant to explain this? Any of this? To my parents, to my sister, to the boys... Only Marissa knew about the original Hand and Flowers incident—not the sordid details of the nature reserve excursion, but that a boy I liked had dumped me by text, and she'd offered to hunt Eis down and kick him in the balls. So that might be awkward. Mum was liable to freak out about his criminal record, Dad would want to know what a man like Eis was doing with a woman like me— which was understandable since I kept asking myself the same question—and the boys had never seen me with anyone but Steven. Alfie would probably be okay with me dating, but I wasn't sure about Harry. When Mum tried to set me up with one of her friends' sons a few months ago, he'd overheard and angrily told her that he didn't want a new dad.

I was still sitting on the stairs when Eis arrived.

"I binned off the meeting. Edie and Bex can cover for me." He handed me a takeaway cup. "You should lock your front door."

"Who's Bex?" I asked numbly.

"My PA. She's been on maternity leave, but we decided it would work for both of us if she came back part-time. You all right?"

"Just...overwhelmed?"

"It's okay to feel that way."

"Really?"

"The past week was life-changing for both of us."

"Life-changing?" I considered that for a moment. "Yes, I suppose it was."

I'd gone from being single and stressed to still being stressed, but in a different way. Now I needed to work out how to coexist with a man I thought I'd lost forever.

"I need to find that little shit who was filming Harry and send him a thank-you card." Eis always knew how to make me smile. He knelt in front of me and leaned his forehead against mine. "Please don't be mad about the roof. I just want you to have a dry house."

"I'm not mad about the roof."

"Please don't be mad about the gate either."

"Why would I be mad about the gate? You didn't make it fall off."

"I ordered you a new one." Oh. "Plus a guy's coming to install security lights. And a new fence."

"You're such a pain in the arse."

"But you love me really."

Love? Did I love him? Teenage me hadn't believed in love at first sight, but that was before I met Eis. Then he disappeared on me, and I thought it was still a load of bollocks. But now I realised there might be some truth in the idea.

"Maybe a little bit. But we're still taking things slowly."

He flashed a grin. "I'll be out of here before the boys get home."

"Thank you." His absence would make things easier. *Keep kicking that can, Janie...* "No, actually you should stay. If you want to, I mean. I'll tell them you're helping out with the plumbing, and if they get used to seeing you around, perhaps it won't be such a big shock when they find out there's more between us?"

Eis pulled me forward onto his knees. "When they realise you're hooking up with the household help, you mean?"

"Something like that." I relaxed into his arms. "I really want this to work."

"It's going to work. Trust me on that."

Thirteen

"Boys, this is Eisen. He's kindly offered to help out with the plumbing. Isn't that great? We might have a shower soon."

"You *will* have a shower soon," Eis corrected.

Harry said nothing.

"I thought he was Chip?" Alfie wouldn't stop staring at his eyepatch. Sheesh. "You said he was called Chip."

"Chip is his nickname."

"Like douchekebab? That's what people at school call Harry. Sophie's brother is in Harry's class, and she told me."

"Is that true?" I asked Harry.

"No," he said, but he was lying. Again.

And Eis knew it too. "Shouldn't fib to your mum, buddy."

"You can't tell me what to do. You're just the plumber."

"Nobody can tell you what to do. But if you want to grow into a man instead of a douchekebab, you'll do the right thing."

Harry stared at him through narrowed eyes, and then his

shoulders slumped. "They call me a douchecanoe, okay? Not a douchekebab."

He stormed off up the stairs.

Great.

That went well.

I looked at Eis, and he looked at me.

"Want me to...?" he asked, nodding towards the stairs.

"Could you just watch Alfie for a few minutes?"

"Sure."

I found Harry spread-eagled on the bed, his face smushed into the pillow. He refused to look at me. I perched beside him, desperately trying to think of a way to make things better.

"Things have been bad at school again?"

No answer.

"How long has this been going on?"

Silence.

"Do you want me to speak with Mrs. Bailey?"

"No!" Then, more quietly, "I'm not a snitch."

"Is Shawn involved in this?"

"No."

"Are you sure? If I'd known what a bad influence he was, I'd never have suggested you go to his house."

"You don't get it." Harry rolled over, and I saw he'd been crying. Shit. "Shawn was trying to help. He said his friends would let me hang out with them, but I had to prove myself first."

"Prove yourself by vandalising someone's property?"

"Prove I wasn't a coward. Then I'd get, like, protection."

"Did it work?"

"No, 'cos I got caught, and now they think I'm crap."

"How did they even know you got caught?"

"Alfie told everyone at his school, so now everybody at my school knows too."

79

Hell, Alfie was turning into the neighbourhood gossip. Why did young boys have to be so mean to each other? Harry had another five years at the comprehensive, and I couldn't let him spend that whole time miserable. I thought back to Eisen's words.

"What do you need?"

Harry looked puzzled. "Huh?"

"What do you need to help make this better?"

"I need for us to move back to Bristol."

Well, shit. I'd walked head first into that one.

"I can't get back together with your dad. He's with Luisa now."

"You don't get it, do you? I don't care about living with Dad; I just want to hang out with my friends again."

The pain in his voice twisted me up inside, and I felt guilty for digging the fragment of a silver lining from the dark cloud of misery. *He doesn't want me to play happy families with Steven.* But we couldn't go back, not when we'd moved to Engleby for a fresh start, for a better life.

"Harry, I wish that was an option. But *I* didn't have any friends in Bristol." Because I'd spent so long working to try to keep us afloat that I had no social life, and the few friends I had managed to make were also colleagues who didn't dare to speak out against Luisa in case they lost their jobs too. "Or a job, or help with childcare, and houses are so much more expensive there. But maybe we could go back for a visit? I've got another driving test soon."

Harry scoffed. "Yeah, right, like you'll pass."

Gee, thanks for the vote of confidence, kid.

"Then we can go on the train. Make a day of it, catch a movie at the cinema, get fish and chips for tea. How about Saturday?"

My children came first. Eis would understand. At least, I hoped he would. If he didn't, that would mean I'd made yet another mistake, and I wasn't sure my heart or my sanity could take it.

A corner of Harry's veil of misery lifted. "Saturday?"

"Why don't you see which of your friends are free?"

Eis did understand. Of course he did.

"Need a lift?" he asked as he packed up his tools. Harry was still in his room, and Alfie was overjoyed because that meant he could watch whatever he wanted on TV.

"I can't ask you to drive all the way to Bristol."

"You're not asking; I'm offering." He gave a mock salute. "At your service. Just tell Harry I'm moonlighting as an Uber driver in my spare time."

Another of those waves of emotion crashed over me, and Eis was the one who wiped away the single escaped tear with a thumb.

"Is my driving that bad?" he asked.

"No, but mine is. I've already failed my test seven times. I'm going for number eight the week after next."

"Is it the parallel parking? I'm shit at that."

"I can do it fine with my instructor. But when the examiner's sitting beside me, I freak out and hit the kerb. Or I forget to look in my mirrors, or I make a wrong turn, or I accidentally break the speed limit. Maybe it'll be okay this time? I still have one more lesson before the big day."

I found myself wrapped in Eisen's arms, his chin resting on my shoulder. There was nothing sexual about it. It was like being hugged by a rock. A tough, impenetrable, overprotective, and weirdly comforting rock.

"If you believe you can, then you will. If you believe you can't, then you won't. That's a quote from Elizabeth

Kennedy-Renner. Did you know she went skydiving on her eightieth birthday?"

"Was she crazy?"

"A bit." He leaned back and grinned. "People say I take after her."

"Have you ever been skydiving?"

"I was right behind her when she jumped out of the plane. There's a video somewhere if you don't believe me."

"Oh, I believe you."

Eis kissed my hair. "I've got a gym in Bristol. It's about time I paid a visit."

"How long since you last went?"

He considered that for a moment. "Sixteen months."

"Wow, you really did go full hermit, didn't you?"

"I haven't been in a great place," he admitted. "They'll be surprised to see me."

"Who's been running the place?"

"I have a great team. Even when I wasn't busy hermiting, I was always training or travelling, so I put in a structure that lets Four Rings run itself."

"Why is it called Four Rings?"

"MMA." He ticked off on his fingers. "Brazilian Jiu-Jitsu, Muay Thai, boxing, and wrestling. Those are the disciplines that a fighter needs to master. There's other stuff in there too, karate and kickboxing, tae kwon do and Wing Chun, but those are the main ones. If Alfie needs something to do while Harry's with his friends, there are kids' classes on Saturday mornings."

"I'm not sure that would be a good idea. He'd probably try to karate-chop Anvil de Witt."

"What's Anvil de Witt?"

"A kid in his class."

"Anvil?" Eis blew out a breath. "Okay then. But

seriously, the first thing we teach kids is that violence is a last resort. Respect comes first."

At least if Alfie was in a gym class, he wouldn't be picking up beetles from the pavement.

"Perhaps he could try a beginner's session?"

"I'll book him a place."

The rest of the week went surprisingly smoothly. Most of the time, I was waiting for the other shoe to drop, but it didn't. I spoke with Marissa and let her know that work on the roof had started sooner than anticipated, and also that the plumbing was going to be cheaper than expected because a chap from the village had offered to help out.

Marissa, of course, put two and two together and squealed through the phone.

"You met a guy?"

"I literally just said that."

"Well, you left a lot of stuff out. No way would he be fixing your pipes unless he's into you. Tell me he isn't another insensitive jerk like Steven?"

"He isn't. He's totally different to Steven." I took a deep breath. "You remember when I was eighteen, I met a guy, and then he did a disappearing act on me?"

"It's him? Ohmigosh, he *is* an insensitive jerk."

"We had...well, not so much a misunderstanding, but he was terrible at communicating in those days. We're both older and wiser now, and I still really like him. Is that crazy? Wait, wait... Don't answer that. I know it's crazy. But we have this chemistry, and I can't stay away."

"If you're just using him for rebound sex, I guess that makes sense. Get it out of your system, that sort of thing."

"I haven't even slept with him. Recently, I mean. He brings me coffee and fixes stuff around the house."

"That's weird."

"Is it? I told him I wanted to take things slow."

Marissa paused before speaking. "Okay, as long as you're just using him for free labour and rebound sex, that could actually be a pretty good deal."

"Right." Wrong. If Eisen vanished on me again, he'd take what was left of my heart with him, but I didn't think he'd do that. For one, I knew his address now. I'd go over there with Harry and turn Twilight's End into a freaking rainbow. "Are you still okay to take me to my driving test?"

I'd kind of thought Eis might offer, but he hadn't, and we weren't at a stage in our relationship where I felt I could ask him for favours. He was already doing plenty as it was.

"The whole of that Tuesday is blocked out in my calendar, and Barbara's covering my shift at Fairfield House. The test is at two thirty?"

My stomach tightened just from me thinking about it. "Yes, but I want to get there early."

"And we can have a celebratory lunch after."

"Maybe."

"Don't be so negative. If I can pass, then anyone can pass." That didn't make me feel better. "Did you see Mum's latest photos?"

Oh, thank goodness, a subject change. "The ones where she dressed up as a cat and Dad looked all bewildered?"

"You don't think he's going senile, do you? Liam said confusion is a natural reaction to Hello Kitty, but Dad's looked puzzled in most of the pictures so far."

"He's fine, honestly. Dad just doesn't handle change very well. Remember when Mum swapped his Yorkshire teabags for green tea because it was healthier, and he drank nearly the whole cup before he asked her to check the 'best before' date?"

"I guess."

We chatted for a few more minutes and then said our goodbyes. Marissa and I hadn't always seen eye to eye, especially as kids, but since the breakup, she'd been an absolute rock. I had a good family, Steven excepted, and more than anything, I wanted Eis to be a part of it.

Fourteen

W hen Harry heard that Alfie was going to take a martial arts class, Harry decided that he also wanted to take a martial arts class, as did three of his friends. Thank goodness Eis's BMW had seven seats. He'd also stuck an Uber decal on the door, the idiot.

Harry proclaimed the BMW "nicer than Dad's car," and I checked Alfie's pockets before he climbed inside. For once, they were empty. Guess he was so excited by the prospect of a gym class that he forgot to bring any of his little friends along for the trip.

For Eis, it was a day off from plumbing. Apparently, the pipes in Marigold Lodge were cheap ones made from thin copper, and impurities in the water had caused pinhole leaks to appear here, there, and everywhere. On Thursday, a guy had shown up and installed a water softener while Eis made him coffee and chatted as if he owned the place, and now Eis was pulling up floorboards and ripping out walls to replace every pipe in the house.

I'd given up arguing.

What was the point?

If I cared to dig into my psyche, which I didn't, I'd have to admit that I liked his constant, mercurial presence. It was only my wounded pride that wasn't happy about the situation.

Eis was quiet on the trip to Bristol. Pensive. The team at Four Rings knew he was coming, but he seemed almost nervous about seeing everyone after so long. I thought I understood. People talked. Rumours started. On my return to Engleby, I'd squirmed as people whispered behind their hands in the convenience store, and that was before Mum and her Rotary club cronies had started their matchmaking attempts.

"We're here!" Alfie bounced excitedly in his seat, and four not-quite-teenage boys rolled their eyes at him.

The gym was in what looked like a converted warehouse on a small industrial estate, and Eis drove around to a staff car park at the rear. The boys had come ready in tracksuits, but Eis was wearing jeans rather than his usual sweatpants. Business casual?

"All right, bro?" A member of staff greeted Eis with a man-hug when we got inside. His name badge said *Darren, Manager*, and his genuine smile said Eis was a friend as well as his boss.

Groups trained on padded mats, at punchbags, and in the half-dozen fighting rings that were scattered throughout the cavernous interior. A handful of men were lifting weights in the far corner, and up on a mezzanine, I spotted the kind of equipment I'd attempted to use in the days before I admitted defeat and accepted that a gym membership wasn't compatible with motherhood and working thirty hours a week. Treadmills, stationary bikes, stair-climbers.

I was busy working out the ratio of women to men,

surprised when it was closer to fifty-fifty than I'd imagined, when one of Harry's friends piped up.

"Hey, our Uber driver's picture is on the wall."

"He's not really an Uber driver," Harry told him. "He's a plumber."

I hadn't paid much attention to the giant panels surrounding us, which were mostly action shots with a few motivational quotes mixed in, but now I realised that Eis was in a fair few of them. If I'd thought about it, I'd have realised it was only natural that he'd feature heavily in his gym's marketing material, but my brain was still futzed, and I was totally unprepared for a twelve-foot-tall sweaty Eisen brooding at me from on high. Did you know that in MMA, the competitors wear obscenely tight shorts? They showed everything. Ev-ery-thing.

His slight smirk told me that he knew exactly what I was looking at.

"Six and a half days," he whispered in my ear.

"Wait, so your plumber fights MMA?" another of the kids asked.

Now Darren looked more puzzled than my dad. "A plumber?"

"He's an uber-plumber," Alfie announced. "He's cleaning my mum's pipes."

My cheeks burned, and Eis just started laughing, the bastard. *Please, somebody kill me now.*

"Janie's a neighbour," Eis clarified. "I'm helping out with some DIY."

"Eisen was also the WPFL champion in the light-heavyweight category three years running," Darren told the boys, and Harry's expression changed. Unless I was mistaken, I saw something that looked a little like awe.

"Was that before your eye fell out?" my youngest offspring asked, and I facepalmed. Dammit, Alfie!

Harry nudged him hard. "You can't say that."

"But he has two eyes in the pictures."

"Alfie, please..." I started, but Eis shook his head and crouched in front of him.

"My eye was damaged in an accident last year. It's still there. It didn't fall out."

"Then why do you wear a patch over it?"

"When I was your age, I wanted to be a pirate. Now I'm living the dream." Eis bent lower to tie the lace on Alfie's trainer. "Ready for class, buddy?"

"Hear all those popping noises?" a voice asked from behind me as Eis and Darren led the boys to a square of mats. A female voice. I turned to find a pretty blonde in a staff T-shirt, Lisa, according to her name badge. "That's the sound of ovaries exploding."

"Mine already burst in a shower of confetti," I said without thinking, but Lisa just beamed.

"He'll make a great dad."

I froze.

A great dad.

I'd been so certain that I didn't want more children with Steven that I'd barely given the tubal ligation a second thought. And caught up in Hurricane Eisen, I'd somehow shoved the whole sterilisation procedure to the back of my mind. But of course Eisen would want kids. Little mini-mes to carry his perfect genes. Heirs to his fortune.

"Yes," I choked out. "Yes, he will."

"It's great to see him looking better. I went to visit him after the accident—you know, to take a card and stuff—and he was so depressed. Like, we were worried he might jump off a bridge or something."

Oh, hell. "I didn't realise things were that bad."

"We had a rota for phoning to cheer him up. You haven't known him long, then?"

"I knew him when I was a teenager, and we ran into each other again recently."

"Well, whatever you're doing, keep doing it. He deserves to be happy."

I hadn't expected Eis to teach the class himself, but he changed into a pair of shorts—not the super tight ones—and gathered the kids around him. There wasn't much actual fighting involved, just shadow-boxing and hitting the punchbags. Plus a lot of talk about how to be a good person with plenty of motivational words and encouragement. The three Bristol lads all wanted to sign up for weekly classes, and now I felt worse than ever because Harry and Alfie wouldn't have that opportunity.

Hell.

"How'd you guys like to watch Darren sparring for a bit?" Eis asked after the hour was up.

Harry's eyes lit up. "With you?"

"Nah, Lisa can kick his a— rear end."

"Eis was gonna say 'arse,'" Alfie said. "I know he was."

"Sorry," he muttered as he herded me away from the mats. "I try to watch my mouth around the kids, but it's been a while. What's up?"

"I don't know what you mean."

"Bullshit." He led me into an office and closed the door. "You've been standing there chewing your lip for the past hour."

"You're great with the boys."

"And that's a problem?" He cupped my cheeks in his hands and tilted his head to one side. "Janie, talk to me."

"I can't have any more kids," I blurted.

That caught him off guard. He opened his mouth, then closed it again before eventually trying, "I'm sorry to hear that."

"And it's my fault. I had my tubes tied after Alfie, and I

never thought I'd get divorced or meet another man or want more children, and...and..."

"Janie, shhh. Can't sterilisation be reversed?"

"Yes, but that doesn't always work. The doctor said I should be a hundred percent sure it was what I wanted before going ahead, and I thought I was because, honestly, my marriage was on the rocks before Steven ever cheated." Great, now I was crying again. "And then I watched you out there, and you're going to make the best dad. So if this is a deal-breaker, I need to know now before I fall any harder."

"Nothing in life is guaranteed." Eis used the bottom of his T-shirt to wipe my face. "I'm also going to make the best stepdad."

"You're...you're okay with it?"

"Whatever path life takes us on, I'm okay with it. You're my anchor, Janie. You have been since the day I met you."

I looked up at him through watery eyelashes.

"Also, my ovaries exploded."

He burst out laughing. "That's my girl. Want me to mind Alfie while you take the other boys to the cinema?"

"You'd do that?"

"He might cramp their style. They were talking about a twelve-rated movie."

"Harry's only eleven."

"When I was twelve, I was borrowing eighteen-rated DVDs from my cousin's collection. That's all part of what turned me into the horny jackass who stands before you today."

He was right on both counts. Eisen Renner was absolutely a jackass, and I could feel the evidence of his horniness digging into my stomach.

"How private is this office?"

"The door locks, if that's what you're asking."

"Then lock it."

I experienced my first Eis-induced orgasm in thirteen years pressed against a filing cabinet with a drawer handle sticking into my butt cheek. He got me off with his fingers quickly, expertly, the whole time whispering filth and promises into my ear. Oh, the promises... I planned to hold him to every single one. He swallowed my cry as I came, supported me as my knees buckled, and shook his head when I tried to slip a hand into his waistband, even though his cock was as hard as granite.

"So you're just going to walk out there like that?" I asked. "People will think you've shoplifted a can of Pringles."

"Fuck."

"I can take care of it if you'll let me."

"On Friday. I want our second time to be special."

"And it will be. But at this moment, I just...want it."

Eis looked furious with himself. "I don't have a condom."

"Do you have any communicable diseases?"

"No."

"Well, neither do I. That was another fun thing I had to check after Steven stuck his pencil dick somewhere he shouldn't have."

Eis cursed under his breath and then he was on his knees, peeling my trousers down and swearing some more.

"You should wear dresses," he told me. "Tight little dresses that I can slide up over your hips."

He finally got one of my legs free and gave up on the other. What did it matter if I was wearing a single shoe and half a pair of skinny jeans? I just wanted him, right here, right now. When he freed his cock and stroked himself a few times, my knees nearly gave out, but he quickly steadied me with one powerful arm.

"You okay?"

"Define 'okay.' Don't tease me, you beast."

With no effort at all, he braced me against the nearest wall and slid inside on a long groan, stretching me until I gasped. It was delicious. I wrapped my arms tight around his neck and breathed him in.

"Janie..." he whispered. "My Janie."

Do you know the best part about being taken hard against the wall by a rabid cage fighter? There was no time to think. No time to worry. No time to overanalyse every detail of the situation. Who cared about cellulite or love handles or belly pooch?

Not Eisen.

He thrust into me hard, strong hands gripping my ass, that mesmerising blue eye boring its gaze into me. He fucked me like he meant it, not because it was Saturday night and he figured he might as well get his rocks off before he rolled over and went to sleep. Eis was hard strength and he was sweetness, he was passion with flashes of pain. Fingernails, teeth, the sheer girth of him. This man blew my mind. The impossible happened and another orgasm built, this one coming from deep inside. I spasmed around him as he came, our bodies perfectly in sync.

I was going to have bruises in the morning.

Hell, I'd be lucky if I could walk.

He lowered me onto shaking legs, one hand on the wall to steady himself because he was feeling it too. This exquisite, overwhelming *rightness*.

"On Friday, you're getting a fancy dinner and a bed," he promised.

"I'd settle for tissues."

His cum was leaking out of me. It was running down my leg and splattering on the floor.

"Shit, I'm sorry."

He pulled out, which only made matters worse, then set

about cleaning me up with his T-shirt. Once he was done, he wadded it up and scored a three-pointer in the wastebasket in the corner.

"You're going to walk out the door without a shirt? What if people guess what we've been doing?"

"You think Darren doesn't already suspect?"

My turn to groan. "Are you kidding?"

"I've never brought a woman to the gym before, and he definitely knows I'm a horny jackass."

I sucked in a breath. "As long as the kids don't find out, that's the important thing. Not yet, I mean. Obviously, I'm going to tell them, but I just need to work out the right way to do that."

"You have lipstick all over your face. Might want to wipe that off."

"So do you."

"I'm tempted to wear it as a badge of honour."

I started laughing. Standing there with one bare foot and jeans around an ankle, with damp knickers and freaking bite marks on my shoulder, I giggled like the teenager I'd once been.

And it was the best feeling ever.

Fifteen

All good things come to an end.

I survived a film about robots followed by dinner at Pizza Palace, and I wasn't even mad when Eis bought Alfie a worm farm while I was at the cinema. The two of them spent Sunday morning setting it up in an empty stable at Twilight's End, everyone just sort of accepting that we'd be spending more time there. Then Harry realised Eis had a gym with a cage and punchbags, and Eis gave him a private boxing lesson. Me? I just watched. Watched and smiled.

Things started to fall apart on Monday.

I knew as soon as Harry walked in the front door that he'd had another bad day. His frown made my heart sink into my boots.

"What happened?"

"Nothing."

"I know that's not true."

"Can we have a Halloween party?"

"A party? Here?"

"It's creepy, innit?"

"It is, but it's also messy and not very safe at the moment. Eis has taken up half of the floorboards."

"Can't he put them back again?"

"Well, I don't know..." I'd barely seen Eis today. He'd been here installing a new shower pump, and I'd had a full appointment book at the salon. Which was great because now I could afford groceries, but I also had no idea how far he'd got with the repairs. As soon as Alfie arrived home from school, complete with three worms in his pencil case, the two of them had taken off for Twilight's End to put the frantically wriggling creatures in their new home while I started making dinner. "Maybe we could just go trick-or-treating?"

"Trick-or-treating is for kids, and it's sooo lame. Kyle Alderman's having a Halloween party."

"Great. Can't you go to that one?"

"No, because I didn't get invited."

Ah.

This was why Harry wanted a party, wasn't it?

"How many others didn't get invited?"

"Like, ten people?"

"In the class?"

"In the year."

And there were four classes in the year, over a hundred kids. What kind of parent let their son do that? I mean, to invite just a handful of kids was fine, but to invite nearly the whole year and leave a few out? That sucked.

How feasible would it be to hold a party for the ten or so who'd made it onto the pariah list? Drinks and snacks, beanbags and a movie? I desperately wanted Harry to be happy.

"Let me talk to Eis about the pipes, okay?"

"Really?"

"We might be able to do something small."

Predictably, my idea of "something small" and Eisen's idea of "something small" were poles apart. This was the man who called Twilight's End a "cottage," so why was I surprised?

"Might be tricky to get all the pipes done by then," he said when he brought Alfie back. "I'm still pretty slow at it. Not sure the roof'll be finished either. But it's not a problem —Harry can have his party at my place."

I pictured a dozen eleven-year-olds running around his immaculate mansion in Halloween garb. Yikes.

"Uh, no. They'd wreck the joint."

"We can put a marquee on the front lawn."

"Oh, sure, just put a marquee on the lawn. Eis, I don't have the money for a marquee. Or the time to ring around and hire one, or the energy to decorate it."

"Bex is back. She can do all that."

"Doesn't she have other stuff to do? I'm sure organising a party for a group of schoolchildren isn't a part of her job description."

"Her job description is broad, and no, she doesn't have much to do this month because, in case you haven't noticed, I've been preoccupied with more important things than work. She's mostly shooting the shit with Edie's PA and bugging me to get a haircut."

"A haircut. You realise I'm a hairdresser, yes?"

"So it's a deal, then? You can cut my hair, and Bex can organise Harry's party. Except he can't just invite the ten kids who got left out. He should invite all of them. Plus his friends from Bristol. And Alfie should invite his class too."

"That's a hundred and fifty people."

"Bex will hire security. Chaperones, whatever."

"We'll also need costumes."

Eis glanced behind him. The boys were nowhere in sight, and he gave me a swift, dirty kiss right there in the hallway.

"We will. And yours is going to be a dress."

Sixteen

Another not-quite-surprise came on Friday. At seven p.m.—half an hour late, as usual—Steven arrived to pick up the boys and congratulated me for finally getting the roofers in. No, that wasn't the surprise, merely the precursor.

"Thought this place would fall down before you got around to fixing it. I don't know why you didn't just buy a flat. There wouldn't be so much upkeep."

"Why do you care? You're not the one paying for it."

"I hope that sister of yours has a good financial advisor. If she wants a referral, I could probably get her a friends-and-family discount."

Was he actually serious?

"She's not your friend, and she won't be family as soon as you sign those bloody divorce papers."

"I'll get around to it. Ready to go, champ?" he called to Alfie.

Nice dodge.

"My solicitor will be in touch again this week. You can't keep shirking your responsibilities."

"I'm taking the boys this weekend, aren't I? And I'm paying for all the petrol to drive them to Bristol and back because you don't have a car."

"I have another driving test next week."

He pursed his lips in that funny way of his, the way that meant he didn't think I stood a chance in hell of passing.

"Good luck."

"Arsehole," I muttered.

"Mum, you're not supposed to say that."

Of *course* Alfie was standing behind me.

Steven herded the boys into his car, and as soon as his taillights disappeared, I called Eis. His BMW pulled into the driveway roughly twenty seconds later.

"What were you doing, waiting around the corner?"

"Yup."

Did he realise how *wanted* those little things made me feel?

"I thought I'd have at least ten minutes. Why are you wearing a shirt and tie?"

"Because I owe you a fancy dinner."

"We're going out?"

"No. Find a dress."

I wasn't really a dress kind of woman. The last time Steven had taken me on an actual date, Alfie had still been in nappies. After a quick scrabble through my closet, I settled on a plain black number that was loose enough to hide my lumps and bumps, short enough to be interesting, and sparkly enough to appear as if I'd made an effort. I teamed it with a pair of heels and decided against tights. I'd waxed everywhere yesterday morning, and Eis had that feral look that meant tights would get shredded anyway.

He nodded approvingly as I walked down the stairs. "Nice. We might not make it to dinner."

"We'd better make it to dinner. I'm starving."

"At least it's nearly ready."

By "nearly ready," he meant that the butler he'd hired for the evening was waiting by the front door of Twilight's End with champagne, the chef was putting the finishing touches to the starter in the kitchen, and a maid was waiting in the formal dining room to bring our plates.

Fancy.

So freaking fancy.

"This is too much," I whispered. No way had Eis ordered this spread through Deliveroo.

"It's not enough."

Rather than sitting opposite me, Eis took his place at the head of the table with me to his right. At first, I thought it might be a bit of a power play, but then I realised he'd done it for access purposes. Far easier for him to run a hand up my bare thigh if it was right there next to him.

"There's someone else in the room," I hissed.

"Don't worry, all the staff sign NDAs."

"You think the paperwork is the problem?"

"You're such a good girl, Janie. I'm going to corrupt you."

"A good girl? I screwed you in a stranger's office last week, didn't I?"

Too late, I realised the butler had glided up behind us with a bottle of red. Dammit!

My cheeks burned while he poured a splash of wine, waited for Eis to swirl and sniff, and then filled our glasses.

"I never understood that swirling thing people do."

"Swirling releases the aromas, and smelling the wine tells you its character."

"My wine's character is best described as 'on special offer.'"

Eis chuckled. "I'll add wine tasting to the list of things

we have to do together." Like a Groupon? "My family has a vineyard in the South of France," he continued.

Of course they freaking did.

"How can this possibly work?" I mumbled out loud.

"I guess either we fly over on a weekend when Steven has the boys, or we go during the school holidays and they can come with us. Not Steven, obviously, just Harry and Alfie. Although there's a nice lake on the edge of the property. Can Steven swim?"

"I meant us. You and me. You own a vineyard, and I root through the bargain bins at Tesco."

"I've rooted through the bargain bins at Tesco."

"Have you?"

"Yeah, I accidentally dropped my Rolex in one of them when I went in to buy smoked salmon and champagne."

"Is that a joke? I can't even tell."

"Yes, it's a fucking joke. I order my groceries online from Sainsbury's. It's my dad who roots through the bargain bins, and he brings home all those little sugar and sauce packets from restaurants too. In my parents' kitchen, there's a whole cupboard full of them, and it drives Mum mad. I don't think they've ever bought a bottle of ketchup."

"Is *that* a joke?"

"No. Janie, if I'd known a good dinner would upset you, I would've ordered a pizza."

"I'm not upset. Just...just intimidated."

"Fuck. You want me to send the staff away?"

I shook my head, and he took both of my hands in his.

"Janie, I only want you to have nice things. I hate that you've been living in a cold, leaky house. Worse, I hate that you've been living in a cold, leaky house while I was two miles away in this place and I didn't even know. We lost thirteen years. Thirteen fucking years. I want to spoil you rotten."

Eisen Renner. All the papers called him the ultimate bad boy, but they never mentioned this sweet side. I could so easily lose myself to this man. Just sit back and let him help with the load I'd been carrying for so long. But what was the catch? There had to be a catch. I already knew he was spectacular in bed, so that wasn't the problem. What, then? It was a question I truly didn't want the answer to.

Keep kicking that can...

I conjured up a smile. "Maybe next time we could order pizza?"

"I'll even let you choose the toppings."

The menu was an A to Z of aphrodisiacs. Oysters and perfectly ripe avocado to start, followed by lamb with asparagus spears, baby carrots, and duchess potatoes, and finally honey-glazed figs with chocolate mousse.

And while somebody else cleared away the dishes, Eis carried me up to his bedroom in the east wing—because of course his house had bloody wings—and feasted on my body. He didn't care about all those little imperfections I spent so long worrying over. He made me feel beautiful.

I even forgot my inhibitions when I rode his cock like a cowgirl, when I sucked it like a lollipop and swallowed every last drop of his pleasure. We were a sweaty mess by the time we collapsed among a pile of pillows and a scattering of rose petals.

And I slept better than I had in years.

Seventeen

In the morning, I woke up before Eis, and in sleep, his eyepatch had shifted. I felt weirdly guilty as I studied the contours of his beautiful face. His bad eye... It was just closed. There was some scarring, faint streaks where the acid must have eaten into his skin, but in the pale sunlight, he looked perfect.

His other eye opened.

Shit.

Busted.

"Uh, good morning?"

"It's okay; you can look if you want to."

"Does it hurt?"

"Not so much now. My eyelid is sewn shut. I wear the patch because it invites fewer questions than having an eye that doesn't open."

"Unless Alfie gets involved, anyway. He has no filter."

"He's a good kid, just full-on."

A real handful, Steven said, and he had no idea how to deal with that. Giving Alfie a games console and expecting him to sit quietly in the corner didn't work the way it had with Harry, so Steven mostly left Alfie to me.

"He loves the worm farm."

"Remind me to drop some leaves in the top later. I promised I would."

"Okay. Do we have plans today?"

"Yeah, we're going for a drive."

"A drive where? To your stately home down the road? To your private theme park? To your beach house?"

"Correction: you're going for a drive, and you can go wherever you want."

"But I don't have a car."

"I got you insured on the BMW."

"Are you kidding? That thing's the size of a tank."

"And it has an excellent safety rating."

"I can't drive that. What if I hit something?"

Eis tucked my hair behind my ear and shrugged. "Dents polish out. You have your test this week, and if you're worried, practice will help. Your sister's taking you?"

"We're going out for lunch afterwards."

"I wish I could be there to celebrate, but I have to go to London." He pointed to his eye. "Checkup."

"You have those regularly?"

"Every month at the moment. When I first woke up in the hospital, I thought that I'd heal up and that would be it, but now I know you never truly recover from an injury like this, and I was one of the lucky ones. I can still see. The plastic surgeons did a good job with my scars." He smiled. "And now I have you."

"You do." A giggle burst out of me. "My parents are gonna shit a brick when I take you to meet them."

"Oh?"

"A hot pirate? Come on. My mum keeps trying to set me up with clones of Steven."

"My parents will probably give you the third degree. 'Who are you and what plans do you have for our son's money?' That sort of thing." Eis gave me a sheepish look. "I've brought home one too many gold-diggers. Nothing serious, and I knew exactly what they were from the start, but Mum still hated it. She'll love you. So will Edie, who would have driven over here this weekend if I hadn't told her to give us some space."

I was nervous about meeting his family, but mostly, I was terrified that something would go wrong before I ever got the chance. What if Eis changed his mind about me? But I put my nerves aside as we took a shower together, which turned into me on my knees with his cock in my mouth. I'd hoped that if I distracted him enough, he might forget about the driving, but no such luck.

We started off trundling around the roads on the estate, which was even bigger than I'd previously thought, and after lunch, we ventured out into the big wide world. He made me drive all the way to Exmoor, where we took Primrose for a long walk and had lunch in a little café. On Sunday, we went to Dartmoor. The boys would have loved it, especially Alfie, but I enjoyed having Eis to myself. Well, almost to myself. Every time he moved in for a kiss, Primrose woofed and ran circles around us.

It was a good day.

A great day.

Then the boys came home, late once again. Luisa was driving, and Steven climbed out to fetch the overnight bags from the boot. At least if Luisa was there, he wouldn't try to come in, which was a relief because Eis was upstairs, measuring the room that would become Harry's so we could order furniture. We'd left the BMW up the road so I didn't have to deal with an awkward conversation this evening.

Only Alfie had other ideas.

"What the...? Steven, what happened to Alfie's face?"

"Don't ask me. He did it while I was out."

"You went out and left Alfie home alone?"

"Luisa was with him."

"Don't worry; it's pen," Harry said.

Alfie turned to face me, and he'd done a thorough job. The black patch covered his entire eye, and he'd even drawn a thin strap going across his forehead.

"I just wanted to look like Eis. Eis is cool."

"Who's Eis?" Steven asked.

"Our plumber," Harry told him, and I could have hugged my darling son. "He's fixing the shower."

"Luisa needs to watch Alfie better. He could have poked his eye out."

"And you need to stop him from bringing woodlice over. It's upsetting for her."

"It is? Gee, that's a shame."

"Janie, we need to act like grown-ups about this."

I stuck my tongue out and walked into the house with the boys following. Steven was such a twat. Was it possible to buy woodlice in bulk? Online or something? I'd have to look into that.

Eis laughed like crazy when he saw Alfie's face. I didn't laugh quite so hard when I realised he'd used Sharpie, and it wouldn't come off, even with make-up remover and an exfoliating pad. The internet suggested using hand sanitiser, but I couldn't get too close to his eye with that.

And while I tackled the Sharpie problem in the bathroom, I could hear Eis and Harry in the bedroom, talking about furniture. Harry wanted a desk and a bookshelf, and then Eis got his laptop out and they started scrolling through the IKEA website.

It made my heart ache, but in a good way. It was so swollen that I thought it might burst. Should I tell the boys that Eis and I were dating? I wanted to, but what if that changed everything? I worried about Harry. The Halloween planning was going well, Eis assured me, and I didn't want to jinx it. His assistant had even arranged for a minibus to come from Bristol with Harry's old friends.

I'd tell the boys in a couple of weeks. Let this relationship settle first.

"We're having pizza," Harry announced. "Me and Eis ordered it. I got you the one with the pepperoni 'cos I know you like that."

"Did you get me the pineapple one?" Alfie asked from his seat on the edge of the bath.

"Extra ham, extra pineapple," Harry said and rolled his eyes.

Guess that meant Eis would be joining us for dinner, and it felt...right. As if we were taking the first tentative steps towards being a family.

"Mum, what's a bailiff?" Harry asked before he bit into his first slice.

"Why do you ask?"

"A guy came to pick up Dad's car, and I heard him say he was a bailiff, but Dad said he was just helping out because the new car's getting delivered next week and they won't both fit on the driveway. But why wouldn't Dad get a new car before he sold the old one? Now he doesn't have a car at all. Anyhow, that's why we were late again. Because we had to wait for Luisa to come back with her car and drive us home."

Home. It made me so freaking happy to hear Harry call it that. For so long, it had been Marigold Lodge, and he'd hated the place. What else made me happy? That Steven was finally facing some consequences for his poor decisions. He'd ruined my credit; now his was suffering too. A visit from the repo man was just what he deserved.

"Maybe Luisa was with her other boyfriend," Alfie piped up. "I don't like him."

Uh, what? "Her other boyfriend?"

"He came over when Dad took Harry to the football, but Luisa told me not to tell Dad, so I didn't."

Eis was trying to keep a straight face, but he wasn't doing a great job of it.

"Why don't you like him, buddy?"

"He smells like that stuff Dad sprays on his armpits, but like, a lot, and he told me I couldn't watch TV and I had to go in my room."

"Chickens coming home to roost," Eis muttered.

More like buzzards circling.

"Can I have a chicken?" Alfie asked. "It could live in the garden at Eis's place."

They both looked at me.

"It'd be good for the boys to learn where food comes from," Eis said.

"I'm not plucking a freaking chicken."

"I was thinking of the eggs."

Right. They both kept staring, and then Harry joined in. Great. I grudgingly shrugged.

"If you look after the worm farm properly, perhaps in a few months we could get a chicken."

Harry shook his head. "I learned about farm animals at school, and chickens don't like living on their own. We have to get at least two."

"We can call them Nemo and Dory," Alfie said.

"No, dumbass, those are fish."

"Harry, don't call your brother a dumbass."

"So we should get fish as well?" Alfie asked. "They can live in the swimming pool."

Eis was trying not to laugh, his eye sparkling. "Let's start with the chickens, buddy. Maybe later, we can put in a pond."

Lisa was right; Eisen Renner made the best dad.

Eighteen

"So, how are things going with Eisen?" Marissa asked.

"Good. Really good. He seems more excited about the party than the boys are."

Tuesday morning, start of the big day. Would it be eighth time lucky? Eis had left for London late yesterday morning with Primrose, and having dinner without him felt weird. But life was good. Not only had Alfie's cast been removed for good yesterday, so he'd stopped complaining about itchy skin, but we also had a working shower at Marigold Lodge. Eis and an electrician had finished installing it yesterday before Eis headed off.

"Do the boys know you're dating him now?"

I nodded. "They're okay with it."

Maybe even better than okay. Mrs. Bailey, Harry's headteacher, had called right after I took a shower with Eis and informed me that we needed to talk. My heart had sunk as memories of my own visits to the headteacher's office came flooding back. How bad would it be?

"Harry's been telling lies," she said. "Here at Southcott

Comprehensive, we encourage honesty at all times, so it's best if we can nip this in the bud now."

"What lies has he been telling?"

"He's been bragging to the other boys that his mother is dating a cage fighter."

He had?

"At any point, did it occur to you that he might be telling the truth?"

"On Harry's application form, you said you were married, and you noted your husband's occupation as 'accountant.'"

Ah.

"Yes, well, I'm separated, and my boyfriend is a cage fighter."

"I see."

"Do you? Do you realise why Harry said that? It's because he keeps getting bullied. Maybe before you start accusing him of lying, you should look at tackling the bigger issue?"

When Harry got home, I asked him about the cage-fighter-dating thing, and he told me he was "eleven, not stupid." Apparently, he and Alfie had been talking, and they figured it would be okay if we all went to live at Twilight's End because who wouldn't want a swimming pool and a movie theatre? Perhaps for the first time in my thirty-one years, one of my problems had resolved itself.

"Liam swapped his shifts around so he can come to the party," Marissa said. "We can stay at Mum and Dad's house overnight. Air the place out a bit before they get back."

"I'm hoping we won't have any medical emergencies, but we will have plenty of wine."

"Should we bring anything?"

"Just yourselves and your costumes."

"I was going to be a cat, but then Liam's sister said she

had loads of old costumes from her theatre days, so now I'm coming as a witch. Serena's friend is a make-up artist, and she offered to help with the tricky bits."

"Why don't you invite Serena and her friend too? The more, the merrier."

"Are you sure?"

"Eis has ordered enough food for two hundred people, and that's not an exaggeration. Invite anyone you want."

"Liam's brother's staying with us for a few weeks before he goes travelling."

"Excellent—bring him too."

I'd never held a party where I didn't have to organise every little thing, and the lack of control was oddly terrifying. What if someone forgot the paper plates? Or there was a problem with the music?

The upside?

I was so busy worrying about the party that I forgot to worry about my driving test. And the two extra days of practice had helped, together with Eis's tips and his "who gives a shit if you prang it?" attitude.

I passed.

I finally passed!

Marissa hugged the breath out of me, and we both squealed in the car park. Strangers gave us a wide berth. Over my sister's shoulder, I saw the look of relief on my driving instructor's face, although no doubt her joy would be tinged with disappointment that I didn't need to pay hundreds more pounds for lessons.

"I knew you could do it!" Marissa said. "No more L-plates."

"Now I graduate to P-plates. I'll probably keep them on forever."

The first thing I did when Marissa released her grip was message Eis.

ME

I passed!

Then I opened a text from Harry.
And the bottom dropped out of my world.

HARRY

Did you see this? He's such a jerk.

The dumb part of me that had flung caution to the wind and leapt into the relationship with Eis hoped that Harry was talking about Shawn, but the chill punching its way up my spine told me the truth. I clicked on the link.

Usually, I avoided the tabloids like the plague, but there was Eis, front and centre on celebgossip.com with a leggy brunette as they strolled along a city street. A small boy with dark brown hair skipped between them, one hand in each of theirs and a huge grin on his face. Happy. They all looked so happy.

Like a proper family.

It was a great picture. Crystal clear.

And the boy had Eisen's eyes.

"I feel sick."

"What happened?" Marissa leaned over my shoulder. "Oh. Yikes."

Spotted in Kensington: Ladies' favourite Eisen Renner finally emerges from his man cave with a stunner on his arm.

Renner refused to answer questions as he headed for brunch with the mystery brunette, but he's in great shape after last year's acid attack. We think the eyepatch only makes him look hotter. Hopefully, Ironman will be back in the ring soon, giving it some pow-pow-pow as we go wow-wow-wow at the sight of those famous butt cheeks.

I knew it.
I knew he was too good to be true.
"Who's the little boy?" Marissa asked.
"I have no freaking clue!"
Another message from Harry.

> **HARRY**
>
> Everyone says that you can't be his girlfriend because he has a new girlfriend. Is it true?

"Is it?" Marissa asked.
"Stop asking questions. Just stop! I don't know. I don't know anything, okay?"

Fingers trembling, I dialled Eis's number, then pressed the phone against my ear as I paced the car park at the test centre. But there was no answer. Had I made another colossal mistake?

In hindsight, I was glad he hadn't picked up because what would I have said? *Do you have a secret child? Are you cheating on me with her, or are you cheating on her with me? Can Alfie at least have his worm farm back?*

I needed time to think things through.

After a not-so-tearful goodbye with my driving instructor, Marissa chauffeured me back home and followed me into the silent, half-finished house. Past Eis's work boots in the hallway, past his coat draped over the newel post, past the bag of sports kit he'd brought for the boys.

"What are you doing?" she asked as I began rummaging through drawers in the kitchen.

"Looking for the corkscrew."

Finally, I found what I was searching for, wrenched the cork free from Tesco's finest bargain-bin wine, and swigged straight from the bottle.

Marissa pursed her lips. "Is that a good idea?"

"Who can say? My judgment is terrible."

This should have been such a happy day, but instead, it had turned into one of the worst of my life. Hadn't I learned my lesson yet? Eis didn't call. Marissa picked Alfie up from school, and Harry stomped off upstairs when he arrived home on the bus. I was just numb. Lying face down on the sofa, numb. Once again, I'd dared to dream of the future, only to get a rude awakening.

I knew I had to speak with him.

Eventually.

I just... If I put it off, maybe I could keep pretending for a while longer?

This wine really did taste like shit.

"Do you want me to stay?" Marissa asked after I'd been wallowing in misery for an hour or possibly two. Perhaps I *should* move back to Bristol? I couldn't stay in Engleby, not with Eisen so close by.

"What's the point?"

"I could make you dinner?" She paused for a moment, and I could feel her staring at me. Judging me. "I'll go and pick something up from the shop. Fish fingers? Spaghetti?"

"I'm not even hungry."

A door slammed. Gravel crunched in the driveway. Marissa drove off, and how much food was she planning to buy? The shop was only a five-minute walk away. Then I heard voices in the hallway.

"Are you the ratbag?"

"Uh, no? I don't think so."

Great. Not Marissa leaving. Eis arriving. Fantastic.

He burst into the living room. "Janie, what's going on?"

"Shouldn't that be my question?" I asked the cushion. "Brunch?"

"You want to go to brunch? It's seven p.m."

"No, *you* went to brunch. I saw a picture on the internet."

"And?"

"With a woman."

"So?"

"And a kid."

"Yes, because my prick of a cousin decided a game of golf was more important than his son."

Wait, what?

I raised my head. "The boy is your cousin's son?"

"Well, he's not mine, is he?"

I slumped back down.

"Fuck, no, you thought he was my kid? Ah, shit." He must have knelt beside me because I felt his breath on my cheek. "Janie, Bex and I took Arlo to McDonald's while Edie looked after the baby. Bex's baby, not my baby," he clarified. "Some movie star rented the house a couple of doors up, and there were paparazzi standing around on the pavement, waiting for a story. Don't believe a word they write. They twist the truth, they make stuff up, they edit pictures. It's all bullshit."

"They said you had a great butt, and I know that part is true."

"Okay, *almost* everything they write is bullshit."

"You didn't answer the phone."

"Yeah, because they don't let you keep it during surgery."

"Surgery?" I scrambled up to sitting and blinked a few

times, and I'd drunk way too much of that wine because Eis was looking back at me. Looking back at me with both eyes. "You didn't say anything about surgery."

"I wasn't sure what was going to happen today. Whether I'd be able to see, or if they'd just sew everything up again. I was really fucking scared," he admitted. "Nine months ago, I volunteered to be a guinea pig for an experimental procedure. Scientists took stem cells from my good eye and grew me a new cornea. Then they grafted it on, and it was a matter of waiting and hoping."

Oh my gosh. He'd had *freaking surgery*, and he hadn't warned me?

"You are *such* an idiot. I could have cancelled my driving test and come with you."

"Which was the main reason I didn't tell you. I wanted to, but..." He laid his forehead against mine. "When I'm scared, I bottle everything up."

"What else is scaring you? What other secrets are you keeping?"

"Nothing, I swear." His gaze locked on to mine. "Absolutely nothing else scares me apart from the thought of losing you. I feel like we can finally have the life we should have shared thirteen years ago."

Maybe I had overreacted a little this afternoon. Eis had told me he was going to a medical appointment, and he'd mentioned Bex a hundred times. Plus taking a young boy out for brunch because his father couldn't be bothered was precisely the kind of thing Eis would do.

The truth was, I was scared as well. It was all too easy to react before thinking, to jump to the wrong conclusion based on fear rather than logic. And the only thing I was scared of was losing him.

I touched a finger to his scarred temple.

"You can see out of your bad eye?"

"Not as well as I used to, but yes. They say my vision should keep improving over the next few months."

Sheepishly, I wrapped my arms around him. "I'm sorry. I'm sorry I was a bitch."

"I get it. This is new. And I also understand why you have insecurities, but I love you, and I'm not going anywhere."

"I love you too."

"Bleurgh." Oops. I'd almost forgotten Marissa was still here. "You two are so sweet my teeth hurt."

"Marissa, meet Eisen. Eis, this is my sister, Marissa."

"Good to meet you, Marissa."

"I'm absolutely not going to comment on your butt." She clapped both hands over her mouth. "Sorry."

"As you can see, putting one's foot in it runs in the family."

"It's true," Marissa agreed. "Is that a 'no' on the fish fingers?"

"We're okay, but thanks."

"Rightio. I should head home. Uh, Eisen? Your car is blocking me in."

"Janie can move it."

"Janie can't. She drank half a bottle of wine." Marissa squinted out the window. "Is that a cat on the bonnet?"

"No, it's a bow."

"Why do you have a bow...? Oh! Ohmigosh! Janie, you definitely have to keep him."

"Because he has a bow? Or are we back to the butt discussion?"

"Because he bought you a car, stupid."

"What?"

"A car! It's super cute."

"He can't buy me a car. Cars are really expensive."

Eis pressed a key into my hand. "Janie, I bought you a car. Get over it."

"Yes, Janie, get over it." Marissa gave me a hug and whispered in my ear. "Don't you dare let him go. And change your top—that one has drool on it."

I changed my top. I also washed two paracetamol down with plenty of water and poured the rest of the wine into the sink. Eis set the record straight with Harry, and we all got an important lesson: don't believe everything you read on the internet.

Eis took us out for dinner in my new car, a tiny red BMW with every extra option available, and when Harry picked up a napkin for a lady at the next table, and she smiled at me and said, "What a lovely family you have," my eyes began leaking over dessert because it was true.

If Steven didn't sign those divorce papers soon, I was going to shove them up his stubborn backside.

Nineteen

"I can't believe you did all this in a week."

Bex beamed at me. "I love parties."

After the misunderstanding, Eis had asked Bex to come to Engleby so we could get to know each other. And she'd brought Arlo, her baby daughter, and her husband, who apparently did something in IT and could work from anywhere. Arlo was Alfie's age, and the pair had quickly become friends.

Arlo was indeed Eis's first cousin once removed. He was also Bex's son. I got part of the story from Eis and the rest from Bex, who absolutely loved to talk.

"Robert told me he was single, the bastard. Took off his wedding band and everything. Honestly, he was terrible in bed, so it's not as if I'd have ever called him again, but then I found out I was pregnant. He gave me a fake number, can you believe that?"

"How did you find him?" I'd asked.

"My friend Cassandra was dating this guy who worked as a private investigator, and he agreed that Robert was a massive prick and tracked him down for free. Of course,

Robert denied everything because that's just the kind of jackass he is. So I tried to get one of those antenatal DNA tests, but the safe one came back inconclusive, and I wasn't going to stick a needle into the placenta and risk a miscarriage. Honestly, I felt so sorry for his wife."

From what Eis had told me, I felt sorry for her too. Robert Kennedy-Renner had lied through his teeth and told anyone who would listen that Bex was a slut who'd probably slept with half the men in London. In reality, Bex was a model who'd made a mistake, and when her body shape changed, she couldn't find work. Eis had given her a job as assistant to his then-PA to keep her off the street.

Fast-forward several years, and Robert was divorced, Bex still worked for Eisen, and everyone hated Robert's guts, including Elizabeth Renner, who'd cut him out of her will entirely. Robert's ex-wife had moved to California, but she still sent Eis a Christmas card every year.

"Normally, I hate parties," I told Bex. "They're always so much work."

Kids' parties were the worst, but even Steven's work get-togethers had been a chore. Sipping Prosecco while my feet hurt, making small talk with boring men who stared at my breasts... But here at Twilight's End, we had an army of professional entertainers, caterers, and cleaners, and I'd come as Arwen from Lord of the Rings, so my shoes were sandals and actually quite comfortable.

"I need to rescue Edie," Bex said. "Hold on a second."

I turned to see that Edie had swapped her tiny beaded purse to her right hand, a prearranged signal that meant "get me out of here." Right now, she was talking with Marc di Gregorio, Hollywood heartthrob and global megastar, who'd tagged along to the party with Serena Carlisle and her fiancé. She'd introduced us earlier—they were busy filming a two-part special of *Whispers in Willowbrook* in the

Cotswolds—and I'd discovered he was also an incorrigible flirt. I wasn't sure he even realised he was doing it.

Edie didn't like flirts. She didn't like men, period. She felt uncomfortable around them, according to Bex, plus she rarely touched alcohol, and she never went out alone. I understood now why Eis had been so ready to punch Neil Short in the face. He'd broken something in Edie that I wasn't sure could ever be fixed.

Across the room, Eis spotted the signal as well, but Bex was already on the move. He headed in my direction instead. Although secretly, I preferred when he was walking away from me—his Captain America costume left little to the imagination, ass-wise.

"Okay?" he asked.

"So okay that I keep having to pinch myself. You don't think the acrobats were a bit much? I'm exhausted just from watching them."

"I guess now isn't the best time to tell you that Harry's planning a Christmas party? He wants an ice rink."

"You're going to let him have an ice rink, aren't you?"

"Probably."

I was gradually coming to realise that Eis was just a big kid himself. He might look hard on the outside, and he could act tough when he needed to, but inside, he was all heart.

We were still mapping out the shape our lives would take. He'd finally convinced me that he wasn't going anywhere, and I'd tentatively agreed that, at some point, we'd move into Twilight's End. I just needed to break the news to my parents first. Mum would undoubtedly lose her mind when I told her I'd managed to fall headfirst into a serious relationship in the time it had taken her to sail from Japan to North America, but Dad would just be grateful he didn't have to help with any DIY. The boys had already picked out their new bedrooms, and Marissa had decided to rent Marigold Lodge out to another family in need of a home. She'd even suggested offering a discount on the rent if there was a cockwomble of an ex in the picture. It was time to pay it forward.

Now that Eis's future looked clearer health-wise, quite literally, he was considering his professional future too. He didn't want to return to the cage full-time, but he did want to teach more, and he wasn't ruling out the occasional exhibition fight. Which I wasn't sure I could bear to watch, but I'd support him in any way that I could. As for me, I'd carry on renting a chair at the salon, but I'd pick my hours carefully. Eis had threatened to book all my appointments if I worked too hard. People said that money couldn't buy happiness, but Eis's fortune could buy time to spend with the people I loved, and that was basically the same thing.

My solicitor had sent another letter to Steven, but we were still waiting for an answer. With Steven's money troubles, I just wanted to sever all ties as fast as possible. I wasn't rolling in it, not by a long shot, but I was careful with the savings I did have, plus I had two safety nets ready to catch me if I fell.

Eisen and Marissa.

My family.

Marissa might have won the lottery, but I was the luckiest woman on earth.

Eis went to keep Edie company, and I stayed to watch the boys. This was all I'd ever wanted—for them to be happy. Most of the kids from Harry's class had shown up in the end, even Kyle Alderman, the boy who'd been holding the other party. Serena had brought three make-up artists along, and they were painting the younger kids' faces, no Sharpie in sight, thank goodness. We had butterflies, pumpkins, clowns, dolls, frogs... The list went on. Harry was a pirate, and Alfie had insisted on dressing up as a spider.

"Ma'am?" One of the men from the security team touched me on the shoulder. "You have a visitor at the gates, but his name isn't on the guest list."

"What's his name?"

"Steven Osman. He says he's your husband?"

Steven? Steven had shown up? How did he even know where I was?

"Tell him to leave, please."

"We did try that, but he says he's here about an important matter, and you'll want to speak with him."

The divorce papers? Could it be the divorce papers? Oh, happy days if it was. This would be the best Halloween ever.

"Fine, I'll speak with him."

Twenty

The conversation with Steven wouldn't take long. It wasn't as if we had much to say to each other. The sooner I was Ms. Taylor again, the better. Obviously, we'd still need to talk about the boys when necessary, but drop-offs and pick-ups were the only time I wanted to see him, full stop.

I trailed the man in black down the driveway, irritation building. Steven was fidgeting in front of a second guard, shifting from foot to foot and glancing around warily. He broke into a grin when he saw me coming. Honestly, I'd thought hiring security was overkill, but now I was glad I'd listened to Eis.

The first clue I got that Steven wasn't bringing divorce papers was the bunch of flowers in his hand.

The second clue was the absolute bollocks that came out of his mouth.

"Janie? Why are your ears pointy?"

"Because it's Halloween?"

"Right, never mind. I've been doing some thinking,

soul-searching if you will, and I realise now that I made a terrible mistake."

"A mistake?"

"I never should have left you. You were everything I wanted in a woman. Everything I needed. A momentary infatuation impaired my judgment briefly, but I've come to make things right."

"I see. Does this have anything to do with your Jaguar getting repossessed and Luisa shagging another bloke behind your back?"

"You know about that?"

"Of course."

"But...but how?"

"The boys told me. It's amazing what you learn if you actually listen to them. Such as the fact that Harry doesn't like football, for example. How did you know I was here?"

"I figured you'd be with Alfie, and his phone's here."

"You turned on the tracking app again?"

I mentally added "acquire new phones" to my to-do list, right above "kick Steven off a tall building."

"It's there for safety."

"Which part of 'safety' involves stalking me at a party?"

"You're my wife. I care."

Give me strength.

"Leave. Just leave. Turn out of the gates and follow the sign for Fuckoffsville, and after you get there, take the turning for Fuckoffsomemore. When you reach the cliff with the big notice that says 'No pillocks beyond this point,' put your foot on the gas, ignore the warning signs the same way you always do, and keep on fucking going." I turned to the security guard who was standing impassively beside me. "I'm so sorry."

"It's quite all right, ma'am."

127

"Janie, that's really childish," Steven whined. "We're still married."

"Only because you keep dragging your heels on the financial settlement."

As he'd done for our entire marriage, he ignored the parts he didn't like and changed the subject.

"Why are you dressed up like that?" He wrinkled his nose. "I can understand the youngsters wearing costumes, but you're at least thirty years old."

Honestly, I wasn't sure whether to punch him or be flattered because I was almost thirty-two.

"At least thirty? Steven, do you even remember when my birthday is? Let's just go for the month here."

"Uh...uh... It's sometime around Christmas... December?"

How had I stayed with this pillock for as long as I did? Every year, he'd forgotten my birthday, and when I'd bothered to remind him, he'd just promised to get me a better Christmas present instead. Two gifts in one. Then he'd arrive home with a sad bunch of flowers or—on one memorable occasion—a giant cookie cake that said *Happy Birthday Julie*. Apparently, the shop had been selling it off cheap after Julie ditched her boyfriend and he declined to collect it. Julie had the right idea.

"Look, I make no apologies if my idea of having fun is juvenile compared to your hobby of porking my boss. If it bothers you, have you tried minding your own fucking business?" This time, the security guard's lips twitched. "Again, I'm so sorry."

"I was in the Navy, ma'am. I've heard far worse."

"Carry on, babe. Your filthy mouth is making me hard."

Oh, shit.

Who had told Eis I was here?

"Who the hell are you?" Steven snapped.

"Eisen Renner." He held out a hand, and Steven shook it automatically because he afforded men a respect he didn't offer women. Ah, that little wince made me smile. "I'm Janie's future husband."

I'm sorry, what?

Eis smiled, and he looked relaxed, but it was fake relaxed. I could feel the tension in him when he slipped an arm around my waist.

Steven's mouth gaped open, and he goldfished for a few moments. But then his expression turned calculating.

"If you two are getting married, does that mean I won't have to pay child support?"

That slimy little shitbag. Money. It all came down to money with Steven. I was so stupid for so long.

"Does it matter?" I asked. "It's not as if you've ever paid a penny anyway."

Eis's fingers dug into my hip as he stared Steven down. "I don't give a fuck whether you pay child support, but you know who will? Your boys. When they're older, and they realise their dad didn't care enough to put a watertight roof over their heads, they'll care. And then they won't be your boys anymore."

Now Steven had turned red. "Is this some kind of joke?"

He thought being a father was a joke?

Eis's death stare turned into a smirk. "It's your move, arsehole."

Three more members of the security team had appeared, and Eis gave them the tiniest nod. One of them stepped forward.

"Sir, we need you to leave now."

I didn't wait around to see what happened. I didn't give even one tiny shit. They could toss Steven into the pool for all I cared, and no, he couldn't swim. Instead, I leaned into Eis as we walked back to the party.

"Future husband?"

"As soon as those fucking papers are signed. You good with that?"

It would be fast.

Really freaking fast.

With Steven, I'd spent hours agonising over the details of the wedding. Pink flowers or purple? Veil or no veil? Should we shell out for a fancy car to take us to the reception? Which photography package should we buy? Would people judge me for being pregnant? And don't even get me started on the seating plan.

With Eis, I realised I didn't care about any of that stuff, or what people thought of me. I just wanted him to be mine, and that was it.

"I'm good with that. You think I should see about getting my tubes untied?"

"Yeah, I do. Your birthday is the twenty-fourth of November, by the way. Just in case you forgot."

I'd told him that thirteen years ago.

With Eisen Renner, the big decisions were the easy ones.

The party began to wind down after nine o'clock. The local kids had been picked up by their parents, and the Bristol kids were back on the minibus, along with two parents who were acting as chaperones. Harry was yawning, and Alfie was hyper and telling everyone who would listen that he was getting an entire flock of chickens.

"We can make a quiet exit if you want," Eis suggested. "I wasn't kidding about being hard earlier, and I've got a better use for your sharp tongue."

"We can't leave our own party. What about the boys?"

"Harry's asleep on his feet, and I can borrow a straitjacket from that guy dressed as Hannibal Lecter for Alfie."

"Is it small enough? What about his extra legs?"

"The straps are..." Eis's attention focused elsewhere. "... adjustable. Who's that guy with Edie?"

I turned to look. "Oh, that's Liam's little brother." Little in terms of both age and stature. Heath was two inches shorter than Liam and best described as wiry. The handbag was still in Edie's left hand. "Is she okay?"

"I think so. Edie started the conversation. She never starts conversations. Is Liam's brother a decent guy?"

"I've only met him a couple of times, but Marissa says he's very sweet. He just got out of the Army." I groaned as Alfie bounced over to Marc di Gregorio and began flapping his arms. "Where did Hannibal Lecter go?"

"You deal with Harry; I'll catch Alfie."

"If I'm too knackered to tell you later, I love you."

Our story wasn't exactly conventional, but I knew one thing was certain: I'd be writing "The End" with Eisen Renner at my side. This Halloween would go down in history as a day to remember.

"Love you too, Janie. Always have, always will."

What's Next?

The Happy Ever After series will continue with Heath and Edie's story in *A Very Happy Easter*.

Edie Renner doesn't date. As well as her own teenage trauma, she carries the weight of stories from a thousand other survivors, tales of wolves in sheeps' clothing and battles fought behind closed doors. Staying single is the safest option. Better to be lonely than be trapped.

Parties are a prime hunting ground for the wrong kind of man, and as a face of the wealthy Renner family, Edie is expected to pull her weight when it comes to social engagements. Weddings, fundraisers, the annual Easter egg hunt—her schedule is groaning, and so is she.

When a lifeline unexpectedly presents itself in the form of Heath Carlisle, her sister-in-law's brother-in-law, Edie breathes a sigh of relief. He'll fix her problems, and she'll solve his. A mutually beneficial arrangement. Just business, nothing more.

Too bad nobody told her heart about the plan...

For more details:
www.elise-noble.com/he

My next book will be the second book in the Planes series, *A Devil in the Dark*...

When casino worker Wren Gillebrand goes missing, there's no evidence of foul play, but her boss, Lucian Blane, knows just how evil humans can be. He is the Lord of the Underworld, after all. Together with Wren's friend Vee, Blane sets out to solve the mystery and get his best blackjack dealer back where she belongs.

All Wren tried to do was help a friend, but now her life is in danger. With survival her only goal and uncertain who to trust, she does the only logical thing: she runs. But with a gang of monsters and the devil himself on her tail, there's only so far a girl can get.

For more details:
www.elise-noble.com/devil

If you enjoyed *A Very Happy Halloween*, please consider leaving a review.

For an author, every review is incredibly important. Not only do they make us feel warm and fuzzy inside, readers consider them when making their decision whether or not to buy a book. Even a line saying you enjoyed the book or what your favourite part was helps a lot.

Want to Stalk Me?

For updates on my new releases, giveaways, and other random stuff, you can sign up for my newsletter on my website:
www.elise-noble.com

If you're on Facebook, you might also like to join Team Blackwood for exclusive giveaways, sneak previews, and book-related chat. Be the first to find out about new stories, and you might even see your name or one of your suggestions make it into print!

And if you'd like to read my books for FREE, you can also find details of how to join my advance review team.

Would you like to join Team Blackwood?

www.elise-noble.com/team-blackwood

facebook.com/EliseNobleAuthor

instagram.com/elise_noble

goodreads.com/elisenoble

bookbub.com/authors/elise-noble

tiktok.com/@EliseNobleWrites

Also by Elise Noble

Blackwood Security

For the Love of Animals (Nate & Carmen - Prequel)

Black is My Heart (Diamond & Snow - Prequel)

Pitch Black

Into the Black

Forever Black

Gold Rush

Gray is My Heart

Neon (novella)

Out of the Blue

Ultraviolet

Glitter (novella)

Red Alert

White Hot

Sphere (novella)

The Scarlet Affair

Spirit (novella)

Quicksilver

The Girl with the Emerald Ring

Red After Dark

When the Shadows Fall

Phantom (novella)

Pretties in Pink

Chimera

The Devil and the Deep Blue Sea

Blue Moon

Blackwood Elements

Oxygen

Lithium

Carbon

Rhodium

Platinum

Lead

Copper

Bronze

Nickel

Hydrogen

Out of Their Elements (novella)

Blackwood UK

Joker in the Pack

Cherry on Top

Roses are Dead

Shallow Graves

Indigo Rain

Pass the Parcel (TBA)

Blackwood Casefiles

Stolen Hearts

Burning Love (TBA)

Baldwin's Shore

Dirty Little Secrets

Secrets, Lies, and Family Ties

Buried Secrets

A Secret to Die For

Blackwood Security vs. Baldwin's Shore

Secret Weapon

Secrets from the Past

Blackstone House

Hard Lines

Blurred Lines (novella)

Hard Tide

Hard Limits

Hard Luck (2024)

Blind Luck (novella) (2025)

Hard Code (2025)

Hard Evidence (TBA)

The Electi

Cursed

Spooked

Possessed

Demented

Judged

The Planes

A Vampire in Vegas

A Devil in the Dark (2024)

The Trouble Series

Trouble in Paradise

Nothing but Trouble

24 Hours of Trouble

The Happy Ever After Series

A Very Happy Christmas

A Very Happy Valentine

A Very Happy Halloween

A Very Happy Easter (2025)

A Very Happy Thanksgiving (TBA)

Standalone

Life

Coco du Ciel

Twisted (short stories)

Books with clean versions available (no swearing and no on-the-page sex)

Pitch Black

Into the Black

Forever Black

Gold Rush

Gray is My Heart

Audiobooks

Black is My Heart (Diamond & Snow - Prequel)

Pitch Black

Into the Black

Forever Black

Gold Rush

Gray is My Heart

Neon (novella)

A Very Happy Christmas

A Very Happy Valentine

Dirty Little Secrets

Secrets, Lies, and Family Ties

Buried Secrets (2024)

A Secret to Die For (2025)